A GRISLY SIGHT

Steele flinched at the sight. In his years on the NYPD Strike Force, he'd seen more dead bodies than he could count, but never one like this. There was a gaping, bloody hole in the center of Gates' chest . . . or where his chest had been. The crushed and splintered rib cage looked as if it had imploded. Bloodstained bones framed the horrible damage within. Steele stared down at the corpse and swallowed hard, his throat constricting, his stomach churning. Torn arteries hung limp and loose inside the bloody, congealing mass that had once been Dr. Phillip Gates.

His heart had been torn out . . .

"Who did this, Higgins?" Steele said. "*What* did this?"

Higgins grimaced tightly. "A cyborg," he said.

KILLER STEELE

J. D. MASTERS

CHARTER BOOKS, NEW YORK

KILLER STEELE

A Charter Book / published by arrangement with
the author

PRINTING HISTORY
Charter edition / February 1990.

ISBN: 1-55773-315-5

Charter Books are published by The Berkley Publishing Group,
200 Madison Avenue, New York, New York 10016.
The name "CHARTER" and the "C" logo
are trademarks belonging to Charter Communications, Inc.

PRINTED IN THE UNITED STATES OF AMERICA

10 9 8 7 6 5 4 3 2 1

For Susan Savage
with special thanks to Marge Sjoden
and Kevin Bishop

1

Lt. Donovan Steele came awake to the sound of a piercing scream. Reacting by instinct, he threw himself out of bed. He was naked, but he was not unarmed. A compensated, polymer/ceramic gun barrel slid out of his forearm through a gunport in the palm of his right hand. A dart launcher extruded from inside his left forearm. The gun fired 10mm. bullets from a 15-round magazine built into his artificial nysteel arm. The dart launcher, fed by a built-in 20-round magazine, was capable of firing titanium-tipped stun or poison darts, launching them hydraulically, or explosive rocket darts that were electrically primed, with a millifuse timed to ignite 20 feet downrange for rocket propulsion out to 100 yards. The weapons systems were slaved to his cybernetic brain, which made them completely thought-controlled. With his built-in laser designator and thermal imaging systems, as well as image enhancement and night vision, Steele could not miss.

But there was no target anywhere in sight.

"Steele?" Raven said, sitting up in bed, her jet-black hair hanging down into her eyes, her voice still thick with sleep.

She saw him standing by the side of the bed, crouching slightly, arms held out before him. His head moved quickly as he scanned the darkness of their bedroom, his eyes glowing with twin pinpoints of red light.

1

"What *is* it?" she said, coming suddenly alert.

He moved over to the bedroom door and listened intently for a moment, his hearing turned all the way up. There was not a sound beyond the door in the penthouse apartment. The only sounds he heard where those of his own and Raven's heartbeats, like deep drums to his amplified hearing, and the heavy sounds of their own breathing. He opened the bedroom door and checked outside.

"What is it? What's the matter?" Raven said, coming up behind him.

They were both naked, but unlike Steele, her slim, long-legged body was not partly constructed out of nysteel and polymer and her flesh was no proof against bullets.

"Stay back!" said Steele.

He went out into the apartment and quickly looked around, then went out onto the balcony. There was no sign of intruders. The city glowed quietly beneath him. He turned and saw her standing just behind him, a 9mm. semiautomatic clutched in her right hand. Most women would have grabbed something to cover themselves with. Raven grabbed a gun. Unlike most women, she was completely unself-conscious about nudity. The years she'd spent as a hooker had inured her to that sort of thing. She was not self-conscious about anything.

"I thought I told you to stay back," he said.

"And hide under the covers while somebody takes shots at you?" she said. "Honey, you've got the wrong girl. What's going on?"

He frowned. "I don't know. I heard a scream. It woke me."

"Maybe it was just another dream," she said.

His nightmares were occurring with increasing regularity. Nightmares in which he relived fragments of experiences that were completely alien to him, and yet, at the same time, hauntingly familiar.

He knew the cause. He knew it all too well. But there was nothing he could do about it. It began when he had been assigned to Project Download, "volunteered" by his chief as a test subject for a government experiment in brain/computer interface. They wanted to see if the knowledge and capabilities he had gained from years of patrolling the bombed-out, lawless streets of no-man's-land could be downloaded from his brain, stored in a computer, and then passed on to another individual who had no experience in such things. It was an experiment aimed at enhancing human learning ability.

They had implanted a biochip into his cerebral cortex, a semi-organic picoprocessor patterned on DNA and grown in a Petri dish, that would enable his brain to communicate with a computer and vice versa. They had then conducted a number of experimental downloading sessions, testing the procedure. In the process, they had acquired a file of his mental engrams. Shortly thereafter, Steele was ambushed in the performance of his duties, shot down by assassins armed with automatic weapons. His torn and bleeding body had been rushed to an emergency room, but he had arrived in a coma, a victim of irreversible brain damage. They were able to keep him alive with life support, but there was nothing further they could do for him.

Enter the CIA, in the person of one Oliver Higgins, the agency executive in charge of Project Download. Steele's body, still on life support, was transferred to the top-secret laboratories in the Federal Building, where the still-functioning biochip implanted in his brain enabled them to download the contents of his mind while multiple teams of surgeons and cybernetics engineers worked round the clock, performing the long and highly complicated series of operations that transformed Steele into a cyborg—part man and part machine.

His arms and legs were replaced with sophisticated nysteel prosthetics powered by a tiny, shielded fusion generator implanted in his chest. His skeletal system was reinforced, parts of it replaced entirely with superstrong, articulated nysteel alloy. Organ transplants were effected to replace those parts that had been shredded by the armor-piercing bullets, against which his body armor had been woefully inadequate protection. Burned over three-quarters of his body by the flaming wreckage he'd been trapped in, his skin was repaired with polymer grafts, indistinguishable from ordinary human skin, but far stronger and highly resistant to bullets. Microminiaturized sensors provided feeling in his artificial limbs and skin. His eyes were replaced with bionic optics. His damaged organic brain was removed. In its place, an electronic brain was installed, encased in a nysteel cranium.

And then they programmed him. Programmed him with the mental engrams they had taken from his own organic brain. His mind, his personality, his identity, his very soul, translated into software and programmed into a cybernetic brain, a computer far more efficient than his human brain had ever been. The result was "Project Steele," an experimental cyborg, a living, breathing prototype of the weapon of tomorrow, the first man in history with a computer for a brain.

But the damage to his organic brain was so severe that a lot of data in the form of mental engrams had been lost. The team of cybernetics engineers, headed by the brilliant Dr. Phillip Gates, had to "debug" the program before it could be loaded into his artificial brain. To do this, they had utilized the mental engram files they had recorded from him previously, during the experiments in which he had participated. But they had also augmented the program with what Dr. Gates called "ancillary data," bits and pieces of mental engram files they had gathered from other test subjects in experiments similar to those that Steele had taken part in. This "ancillary data" had been integrated into Steele's engram matrix, meant only to augment his emotional responsivity and nothing more. . . . But in fact, it did a great deal more.

The first dream hadn't even been a nightmare, really. There was nothing to it that would have frightened anyone, but Steele awoke from it feeling chills running down his spine. He had dreamed it was a warm, sunny day and he was with his family in the park. He didn't know which park it was or even in which city. It had seemed familiar, yet it wasn't. His wife was laying out their picnic lunch on the blanket while their children were playing with the dog. It was a pleasant and bucolic scene— only there was something wrong with it. They never had a dog. Steele's ex-wife, Janice, was a blonde. And this woman was brunette. They had two children, Jason and Cory. But in the dream, there had been three, twin boys and a girl. They called him Daddy. And yet Steele did not know them.

The dream recurred. Each time, something new was added. Some new element. He remembered that the woman's name was Donna. Donna what? He didn't know. She was not his wife. She did not look anything like his wife. And yet he felt he had been married to her. It was crazy. In subsequent dreams, the scene became even more surreal . . . and more horrifying. His mother appeared in them. The children were playing in the park when suddenly, with the abruptness of a camera cut, it was dark. Late evening. And Steele's mother had appeared from out of nowhere, looking exactly as she'd looked on that fateful day when she had come home contaminated by a blood sample from the hospital where she had worked, infected with the deadly Virus 3, a terrifying legacy of the Bio-War. She was a screamer.

She had burst through the door of their apartment, her mind already driven insane by the disease, her clothing torn and shredded, her face and body a hideous mass of suppurating sores. She had kept screaming, *My children! My children!* over and over again as she descended on Steele's two younger brothers, sweeping them up into her arms and covering them with deadly kisses . . . and then she'd started biting them. By the time Steele's father got her off them, they were already infected. He had struggled with his psychotic wife, who fought him with terrifying savagery. He finally shot her with his .45, but not before she had infected him as well. With grim determination and tears in his eyes, Steele's father had said goodbye to him, then shot his two infected sons and turned the pistol on himself.

And, just as in real life, in the nightmare, Steele's mother had descended on the children—only not his brothers, but the three children in the dream—and as the woman who was his wife, yet not his wife, screamed in terror, Steele woke up, gasping for breath and trembling violently. Each time it was the same. Memories of his own past overlapping with those of someone else's. Whose? He didn't know.

There was another dream. He was a young soldier, stationed

at an agro-commune in upstate New York, standing guard duty over a cornfield, protecting it from raiders. Steele had never been in the army. He had never been to upstate New York. He had never even seen a cornfield. He had lived in the city all his life. Yet in the dream, he was there, standing on the far edge of the field, listening to the wind rustling through the corn-rows, occupied by thoughts of lust for the young farmgirl who had snuck out to see him in the middle of the night. He had set his assault rifle down against the fence while they flirted and smoked cigarettes, and then she came into his arms and they sank down to the ground, kissing passionately and exploring one another's bodies, and then she straddled him as he lay down on his back, her firm young breasts bouncing as she thrust against him. Then there was a sharp, hissing noise and a sound like a hammer striking meat and a triangulated steel arrowhead came bursting through her chest. Blood spattered down on him as she grunted and fell forward on his chest, the arrow protruding from between her breasts piercing his skin. Horrified, he rolled her off him and scrambled for his rifle with his pants down around his ankles. The first bullet took him in the shoulder as the raiders opened fire. . . .

That was all. Each time, Steele awoke at that point of the dream. Each time, his cries of terror woke up Raven and she was there to hold him, to reassure him, to provide a tangible reality for him to cling to . . . yet the dream was real, too. It had happened. Not to Steele, but to someone else. Someone who had been that young soldier and who had to have survived that raid in order for his memory to have become part of Steele's engram matrix. For that was what was happening. That "ancillary data" used to supplement his engram matrix had started to express itself through his subconscious.

In his dreams, he was reliving parts of other people's lives. Memories and experiences that weren't his, yet that were now a part of him, floating somewhere in the programming of his cybernetic brain. A part of him, now, had *been* that soldier, had made love to that girl and seen her die. A part of him had once been married to that women named Donna. His mind was being haunted by cybernetic ghosts, fragments of other people's personalities. And there was nothing he could do about it.

He didn't dare tell Oliver Higgins or Phil Gates. He was afraid to trust Dev Cooper, the project psychiatrist. He knew only too well what their response would be. They would consider the dreams to be "glitches" in his programming, and they would bring him in, put him on downtime and proceed to debug the engram matrix, to erase the ghost personality fragments from his mind. Only what *else* might they erase in the process?

The science of psychocybernetics was still in its infancy and Steele was its first progeny. There was still much they did not know. They had not known about the effects of the ancillary engram data. They had not, *could* not have foreseen it. And though his personality had been translated into software, the subconscious was a far more complicated thing than even the most sophisticated artificial intelligence computer program. It was like a vast and incredibly intricate spiderweb. Touch one strand, and all the others quiver. *Break one.* . . .

If he allowed them to debug his engram matrix, Steele knew that he might not come out the same. They would undoubtedly rewrite the program in a way that would allow him to still function, but how much of himself would he have lost? Already plagued by doubts about his own humanity, Steele was determined to hang onto his identity, whatever he had left of his own soul, at any cost. He was afraid to tell them what was happening. Afraid of what they'd do. Somehow, he'd have to exorcise these cybernetic ghosts all on his own. Or find a way to come to terms with them. The trouble was, he had no idea how.

He stood naked on the balcony, feeling the warm breeze through the sensors in the polymer skin of his artificial limbs and through the pores of the natural, organic skin on his face, his buttocks, and in the area of his groin. That had been one of the first things Raven had been curious about when they had met. Yes, he had told her, it was "real," a reality she eventually explored quite fully, to discover to her amazement one of the hidden benefits of a man who was part flesh and blood and part computer. She lowered the gun and put the safety back on.

"Only a dream," she said. "That's all it was."

Steele shook his head, uncertain. "Maybe. I don't know. It was so real. . . . I *heard* it. Distinctly. A man's scream."

He went back inside the apartment and picked up the phone.

"What are you doing?" she said. "Who're you calling this time of night?"

He hesitated, still holding the phone. "Maybe I'd better call down to security," he said. "Check with them, just in case. . . ."

"There's nothing wrong," she said. "It was only a dream, that's all. Look, if anything was wrong, we would've heard from them by now."

"Maybe you're right."

"Come on," she said, coming up to him and rubbing his chest lightly. "Relax and come to bed."

"I suppose you're right," he said. "The damn nightmares are so real . . . Still, it can't hurt to check, just to make sure. It'll only take a second."

He punched the number for the security desk downstairs.

"Security." The voice sounded tense, abrupt.

"This is Steele," he said. "Is everything all right down there?"

"I was just coming up to see you, sir," the security man said.

"What is it?" Steele said quickly.

"There's been an alarm at project headquarters," the security man said. "I don't know what it is. They tried to call you just now, but your phone was off the hook, so they called me and—"

"I'm on my way," said Steele.

"Wait," said the guard quickly. "They're sending over a chopper to pick you up. It should be there any minute."

"Right," said Steele, hanging up the phone. "Christ, I should've realized. . . ."

"What is it?" Raven said, seeing the expression on his face. "What's the matter?"

"Something's happened at the project labs," he said, as he

rushed back into the bedroom to get dressed. "That scream I heard was no dream. It must have been Gates. He was trying to reach me through the broadcast link and something happened. Something terrible. They're sending over a chopper for me right away."

"I'm going with you."

"No, you stay right here, where it's safe," he said. "They wouldn't let you down there, anyway. You haven't got the clearance."

He zipped up his jumpsuit.

"Call me the minute you find out what's going on," she said. "Don't make me sit here worrying. You hear me?"

"I'll call you as soon as I can," said Steele.

He heard the sound of chopper blades as the helicopter came in to the penthouse helipad. Christ, he thought, what the hell could have happened down there? Whatever it was, he'd soon find out. He kept thinking about that awful scream. And how it was cut off, abruptly.

The chopper landed on the helipad on the roof of the Federal Building, once the headquarters of the United Nations in the days before the Bio-War. It had been a war not so much of nation against nation as of man against disease and man had lost. Somehow, a group of Islamic terrorist fanatics had gotten hold of a genetically engineered biological agent, and airborne virus created in a lab, and in an effort to bring the western powers to their knees, they had released it simultaneously in several major cities in North America and Europe. However, they had vastly underestimated its virulence and the incredible speed with which it would spread throughout the world. Billions had died in a matter of days. The human organism had absolutely no defense against it. The major superpowers, each thinking the other responsible, had immediately ordered retaliatory strikes, but only a small portion of their nuclear arsenals were actually launched as missile-control personnel keeled over at their posts.

Within days, the population of the world had been reduced to a mere fraction of what it had once been. Governments collapsed. Anarchy reigned. Both Washington, D.C., and Moscow, as well as a number of other major cities throughout the world, had been nuked right off the face of the earth. There were still radioactive hot spots throughout areas of what had once been the United States, Europe, and the Soviet Union. The missile strikes in California had triggered off devastating earthquakes, but the loss of life brought about by the aborted nuclear exchange was nothing compared to that caused by the plague.

Humanity would have been wiped out completely had not the virus started to undergo a rapid series of mutations. A fortunate few had somehow managed to acquire an immunity, but countless others had succumbed before the virus finally mutated into a relatively harmless organism that posed a threat only to the very old and weak, those whose immune systems no longer functioned properly.

Billions had succumbed not only to the virus in its original form, but to its succeeding incarnations, one of which attacked the myelin sheaths of the nervous system, resulting in a progressively crippling disease that left its victims gradually wasting away. Another resulted in the deadly Virus 3, the disease that had produced the screamers. A carrier population of victims that was left physically and mentally ravaged by the disease, screamers were hopelessly psychotic. They attacked anything that moved and they were highly contagious. Those of their victims who survived became infected, turning into screamers themselves within a matter of hours or even minutes, driven stark, raving mad by the disease and breaking out in hideous, festering sores as their bodies literally rotted away. One screamer could create hundreds more before the disease finally consumed him and the police and armed citizenry shot them down on sight. But though the carrier population had been cut down severely since the war, the disease proved stubborn to eradicate. Many of its victims still ran amok like howling beasts out in the countryside and in the lawless, devastated sections of the cities known as "no-man's-land," where outlaw enclaves and para-military street gangs ruled the turf, and the beleagured population struggled for survival in a dark and savage urban jungle.

Such was the world in which Steele functioned as an agent of the weakened and woefully decentralized federal government, with headquarters in New York's Midtown, an embattled nucleus of a city bordered to the north and south by no-man's-land. The Federal Building, which had once flown the flags of all the countries belonging to the United Nations, now flew the state flags of the crippled U.S.A., all save Texas, which had left the union to form its own republic with its capital in Dallas. The Federal Building now housed the offices of legislators and government agencies. What had once been the General Assembly Building now housed the Hall of Congress, where the elected representatives faced the seemingly insurmountable task of uniting the country once again as modern civilization slowly staggered back from the brink of oblivion.

As Steele took the elevator down from the roof of the building to the maximum-security sub-basements, he was escorted by a group of federal security agents armed with pistols and automatic weapons. They stood beside him in the elevator, silent and impassive, but their faces were all drawn and tense. Steele knew better than to ask what had happened. If they even knew, precisely, they would not be authorized to tell him. He did not stop on the 22nd floor, where the administrative offices of the project and the CIA were, but continued straight down to the basement, where he passed a security checkpoint and changed to another elevator that would take him down to the maximum-security sub-basement levels.

On level B–3, he stepped out of the elevator and into what looked like the interior of a concrete bunker. The first things he saw were the dead bodies of Marine guards, not uniformed in full dress or security blues as were the rest of the soldiers in the building, but in full combat gear. They lay scattered about like so much chaff, their bodies torn and broken. Blood was everywhere, in large puddles on the floors and splattered on the walls and ceilings. Steele caught his breath at the grisly sight.

The guards quickly escorted him out of the elevator and past the security station, where there were more bodies on the floor and draped over consoles. The massive, steel-barred door that gave entrance to the underground laboratory complex was a torn and twisted wreckage. Steele stared at it with disbelief. What in God's name could have *done* that?

Adrenaline surging through his system, he hurried down the corridor. The walls were chipped and bullet-scarred, shattered and blackened from grenade explosions. Bodies. Bodies everywhere. And blood. So much blood. . . .

The heavy steel door to the main laboratory complex lay on the floor, ripped off its hinges. And the lab complex itself was a shambles. Heavily armed security guards bustled back and forth along with white-coated lab and medical personnel. It was pandemonium. Flames licked from ruined electronic equipment as lab personnel shot them with fire extinguishers. Sparks shot out from smashed computer banks and consoles. And there were more bodies, lying sprawled out on the floor, draped over pieces of equipment in impossibly twisted positions as if they had been hurled there.

Steele's first thought was a hit. A well-organized, heavily-armed assault team. But *who? How?* To his knowledge, only the outlaw enclaves on Long Island could have mustered up a force and weaponry sufficient to the task. In the aftermath of the Bio-War, organized crime had gone truly bigtime. Not long ago, Steele had led an assault upon the enclave of the powerful Borodini family out in Cold Spring Harbor. Victor Borodini and his sons had led the most powerful of the criminal enclaves. He dealt with the Brood, the heavily armed biker enclave out in Montauk who supplied them with necessities from their agro-commune and fishing fleets. He traded with the freebooters who roamed the Atlantic coast and the Caribbean, supplying them with drugs and ordnance. The Borodinis had even extended their criminal operations into the city, bringing most of the gangs in no-man's-land under their control.

Their enclave had been heavily fortified, protected by armed mercenaries, shore batteries, mines planted around the grounds of the estate and in the harbor, automated defense systems and surface-to-air missiles. And the people who had gone to the

Borodinis for protection provided an added measure of security, rendering any kind of tactical strike impossible without significant loss of innocent life.

Steele had infiltrated the enclave and sabotaged their defense systems, allowing an assault force to come in by chopper, but though the enclave had fallen, Rick Borodini had taken a group of federal legislators hostage, and in order to secure their release, it had been necessary to trade the prisoners, including Victor Borodini and his youngest son, for the hostages.

Could this have been the work of Victor Borodini, a payback for the assault upon his enclave? Perhaps, Steele thought, but if so, then why were there no indications of it on the outside of the building and its grounds? How could they have gotten past the exterior defenses, past the heavily armed security force inside the building and down to the maximum security levels without any sign of struggle?

No, thought Steele, as the guards conducted him through the wreckage of the lab complex, whoever or whatever had caused all this had come from the *inside*, from within the lab itself. What the hell had they been *doing* in here?

He stopped suddenly as two guards came by carrying a stretcher. It was covered with a bloody sheet, but the sheet had slipped enough to show the body's face. It was Dr. Phillip Gates.

"Wait," he said.

He pulled back the sheet.

He flinched at the sight. In his years on the NYPD Strike Force, he'd seen more dead bodies than he could count, but never one like this. There was a gaping, bloody hole in the center of Gates' chest . . . or where his chest had been. The crushed and splintered rib cage looked as if it had imploded. Bloodstained bones framed the horrible damage within. Steele stared down at the corpse and swallowed hard, his throat constricting, his stomach churning. Torn arteries hung limp and loose inside the bloody, congealing mass that had once been Dr. Phillip Gates.

His heart had been torn out.

Steele dropped the sheet and turned away. The guards led

him toward the back of the lab complex and into a windowless, wood-paneled office with thick carpeting and a long conference table in the center of the room. Higgins was there, along with some senior military staff officers and agents.

Dev Cooper was there as well. He was shouting at Higgins as Steele came into the room.

All activity came to an immediate halt. A thick silence descended. "Steele. . . ." said Higgins, turning to him.

"What the hell happened here?" asked Steele.

With the exception of Dev Cooper and Higgins, they were all looking at him strangely. He had seen that look before. He knew it all too well.

"Everybody out," said Higgins.

They hesitated.

"Out, I said!" shouted Higgins. Steele had never heard him raise his voice before. He had never seen the icy, unflappable Higgins lose his self-control.

They all hurried toward the door.

"Not you, Cooper," Higgins said. He took a deep breath and let it out slowly. "Please. I'd like you to stay for this."

"Jesus Christ, Higgins," Steele said, "what's going on? What the hell happened?"

"Sit down, Steele."

Higgins glanced up at the guards and said, "Leave us. Shut the door. I don't want to be interrupted."

Steele glanced from him to Cooper. The psychiatrist looked terrible. There were deep bags under his eyes. He looked as if he hadn't slept in days.

"There's been . . ." Higgins groped for the right word. ". . . an accident," he finished lamely.

"An *accident*?" said Cooper. "Is *that* what you call it?"

"Doctor, please. . . ."

Cooper sat down at the table and took out a pack of cigarettes. He lit one with a trembling hand.

"Who did this, Higgins?" Steele said. "*What* did this?"

Higgins grimaced tightly. "A cyborg," he said.

Steele stared at him. "What?"

"A cyborg," said Dev Cooper, tensely. "They built themselves another cyborg. Only this one went berserk. Ran totally amok. He killed both Dr. Gates and Dr. Gold. Dr. Nakamura's in the hospital, in critical condition. It doesn't look as if she's going to make it. Half the project team is dead, the others are all either severely wounded or in shock. He went through the lab like a one-man demolition crew and then broke out. The soldiers couldn't stop him. He slaughtered everyone who tried getting in his way."

"He escaped through the shuttle platform on level B-1," said Higgins. "Jumped down onto the tracks and broke through into one of the sealed-off, connecting subway tunnels. There's no telling where he may have gone from there. The old subway system runs all throughout the city. Most of those tunnels haven't been used in years."

"He could come up anywhere," said Cooper, wearily. "Anywhere in the city. And he's stark, staring, raving mad."

2

"We were only waiting for the funding to go ahead with it," said Higgins. "We had the team assembled, we had a candidate, everything was ready to go, only we didn't have the funds until you hit the Borodini enclave and we took it down. They were so impressed with your performance that they okayed the funds within two days after the story hit the press. The media was playing it up big, and Gates and I had no trouble convincing them to go ahead with the next phase of the project."

"The next phase?" said Steele.

"Project Stalker," Higgins said. "The first of a new generation of cyborgs. The eventual goal was to have at least one cyborg assigned to each urban Strike Force unit, and then start production on cyborgs for the military. One cyborg could do the work of over a dozen, two dozen men. It would enable us to free up a lot of manpower to get the cities and especially the outlying provinces back under control, establish new agrocommunes and industrial facilities with the people to protect them, do something about the shortages and the lawlessness and start pulling this country back together once again.

"And with more funding for the ongoing work on Project Download," Higgins continued, "we'd be able to produce more biochips, allowing more people to interface directly with computers, programming them with knowledge that would

save years and untold effort and expense. We'd be able to turn
out trained police and military personnel within a matter of
hours. Produce highly skilled technicians in a matter of days.
Scientists in only a few weeks. It would be an incredible step
forward for the entire human race! Think what we could
accomplish! But the damn legislators were dragging their
heels. They wanted to be certain that the process was per-
fected. They were paranoid as hell about the media getting out
of hand and screaming, 'Mind control!'

"They wanted to make sure they had public support behind
them," Higgins said, "so they wanted to go ahead with the
cyborg project, because it was more visible, more glamorous.
But they wanted to proceed slowly. First you here in Midtown,
then Stalker, who was slated for assignment to the Boston
Strike Force, then another one, taking it in easy steps, getting
the public used to the idea before they sprang the concept of
people interfacing with computers on a mass scale. Technology
still scares the hell out of most people. They haven't forgotten
the Bio-War. Until you took down the Borodini enclave, Gates
and I had to fight the Finance Committee for every last red
cent. You helped us turn it all around. The news media loved
you. You were a hero. They voted us a budget in record time.
And now this has to happen. It's a disaster. An absolute
disaster."

"What happened?" Steele asked. "What went wrong?"

"Stalker went insane," said Higgins, wearily. "I don't know
why. He started acting strange as soon as he was brought on
line. At first, Gates thought it was just a normal stress reaction,
much like you had when you first came out of your coma to
discover that you had a computer for a brain. It seemed
perfectly understandable. Something like that can be one hell
of a shock. Stalker didn't take it well. But there was much
more to it than that."

"Were you in on this?" Steele asked Cooper.

Dev shook his head and lit up another cigarette. He had been
a non-smoker when he first arrived from Los Alamos to join
the project. Now, he chain-smoked endlessly.

"I only just found out about it," he said, "right after Stalker ran amok." He looked at Higgins. "Damn it, Higgins, you should've told me! You should have brought me in on this! I might've been able to do something to prevent it!"

Higgins shook his head. "I'm afraid I couldn't do that, Doctor."

"*Why*, for God's sake?"

"I'm not at liberty to go into all that now," said Higgins, "but rest assured, we will discuss it later. Right now, the most important thing is for Stalker to be neutralized before he can cause any more damage."

"And that's where I come in, is that it?" Steele said.

"Yes, that's where you come in," said Higgins. "You've got to find him, Steele. You've got to find him and take him out. You're the only one who'd stand any chance against him. You saw what he did out there. It'll take us weeks to repair all the damage. People have died. Valuable equipment's been destroyed. Priceless data has been damaged, perhaps lost irretrievably. And there's no telling what he'll do now that he's loose out there somewhere in the city. He's death on two legs. He could take out an entire Strike Force unit without even breaking a sweat."

"He's that good?" said Steele.

"Oh, yeah," said Higgins with a grimace. "He's that good. He was designed to be."

"Tell me about him," Steele said. "What's he got?"

Higgins looked at him for almost a full twenty seconds, then looked down at the table.

"I don't know, exactly," he said.

"What the hell do you mean, you don't *know*? What are his capabilities? What kind of weapons systems did you put in?"

"I can only tell you some of it," said Higgins. "He was so new, I hadn't yet been fully briefed on his updates from the original design. Hell, I'm only the project administrator, Steele. Gates was in charge of the design team. Thanks largely to you, we'd received more funding than we had expected and he and Dr. Gold had incorporated a number of improvements into the original design. I don't know exactly what they did. And they can't tell me. They're both dead."

"What about the team that put him together?" asked Steele.

"Dr. Nakamura was in charge of the surgical team that worked on him," said Higgins. "And she's in the hospital, in critical condition. We don't know if she'll pull through. We're trying to get the other members of the team back together for a full debriefing, but that will take a while. And we can't waste any time."

"What about the files?" Steele said. "Gates and Gold surely kept files on what they were doing."

"You saw what it looked like out there," Higgins said. "Over half the equipment's been destroyed. Gates always entered his files directly into the databanks. He never kept anything on paper. It'll be days before we can completely clean up that mess out there. And weeks, perhaps months, before we can reconstitute the data. Assuming we can even recover it in the first place."

"So what you're telling me is that you've made yourself another cyborg, but you don't know exactly what his capabilities are or what weapons systems he has?" said Steele.

"Yeah. I'm afraid that's about it," said Higgins.

Steele let out a long breath. "Terrific," he said. "So I've got to stop him somehow without knowing what he's got. And since he's a new and improved model, odds are he can take me, right?"

Higgins moistened his lips nervously and nodded. "I'm afraid so, yes. However, there are one or two things about his weapons systems I *can* tell you, based on reports from the survivors. He's got a built-in laser turret in his left arm and his right arm fires plasma charges."

"*Plasma charges?*"

"That's how he knocked out most of the equipment," Higgins said. "Gates and Gold apparently went all out. They wanted to show what we could do given the resources. They incorporated state-of-the-art technology and then some."

"Jesus Christ," said Steele.

"Can't we update Steele to match Stalker's capabilities?" asked Cooper.

"How?" said Higgins. "Stalker wrecked the entire complex.

Gates is dead. Gold is dead. Nakamura may not pull through. We've lost most of our equipment and our files, and Stalker slaughtered over half our personnel. It'll be weeks before we can put it all back together again. And it'll eat up our entire budget. We simply don't have the time, the ability or the resources. We can get some help from Strike Force, but aside from that, Steele's going to have to make do as best he can. But you've got to take him out fast, Steele. We've got to try to avoid any publicity on this."

Steele grimaced wryly. "How the hell do you figure on doing that?"

"I don't care how you do it," Higgins said. "I'll call Chief Hardesty at Strike Force headquarters and tell him that this is a top priority, top-secret government operation and you're to have carte blanche in conducting it. But we've got to try to keep a lid on this somehow, or it could ruin everything we've worked for."

"I've got to have a little more to work with," Steele said. "For one thing, I don't even know what Stalker looks like."

Higgins took a deep breath and let it out slowly. "Yes, you do. You know him. Or at least, you knew him once, before he became what he is now."

"What are you talking about?" said Steele, frowning.

"He's your old partner, Mick Taylor."

Dev Cooper gave a start and stared at Higgins with astonishment. Steele suddenly felt his guts turn to water.

"That's impossible," he said. "Mick Taylor's dead. He was killed when Borodini's men ambushed us in no-man's-land. I *saw* him die!"

"No," said Higgins. "He's still very much alive. We were able to revive him, though there wasn't much left to revive. His entire body was riddled with shrapnel and he was very badly burned, even worse than you were, but we managed to keep him alive on life support until we had the funds to begin the reconstruction."

Steele gaped at him with disbelief. "You mean to tell me that all this time, Mick has been alive? *Here*?"

"That's right," said Higgins. "We had him sequestered on

the level below this one until we were ready to proceed with the project."

"And you didn't *tell* me?"

"There was no need for you to know. Besides, we didn't know if we were going to get the funding. It was touch and go. He could have slipped away from us at any time."

"You bastard," Steele said. "You rotten son of a bitch. The man was my partner! My best friend!"

"*Was* your partner, Steele," said Higgins. "He *was* your best friend. The Mick Taylor you knew doesn't exist anymore. There's only Stalker. And Stalker is a dangerous, homicidal maniac. A machine out of control. A deadly machine. A machine that must be stopped."

"By another machine—like me," said Steele.

"I didn't say that."

"You didn't have to."

"My God, Higgins," said Dev Cooper, "didn't it even occur to you that—"

"That'll be enough, Doctor," Higgins snapped. "You and I have plenty to discuss, but this is not the time. Steele, I want to make absolutely certain that you understand the situation. The cyborg that you're after is *not* Mick Taylor. The man you knew is dead. You saw what he did out there. Would Mick Taylor do anything like that?"

"No," said Steele, softly. "No, he wouldn't."

"Then you have your assignment," Higgins said. "Use whatever resources it takes. Get Strike Force to help you on this. You know the men, you can pick your own team. But Stalker *must* be stopped. At any cost."

"Right," said Steele, getting to his feet. "I need to use a phone. I have to call Raven. Let her know what's happening."

"There's no need for her to know about this. Security is—"

"Oh, screw security," Steele snapped. "Without Raven's help, we would never have pulled off the assault on the Borodini enclave. I trust her. And if that's not good enough for you, that's just too damn bad."

"All right, all right, don't get your back up. I'll have

security escort you upstairs. You can use a secure line in my office. I don't want any leaks."

"*Leaks*?" said Steele. He snorted derisively. "Within twenty-four hours, you'll have the media all over you. There's no way you'll be able to keep something like this under wraps. They'll be on you like a fox on a duck, Higgins, and you'd better be ready with some answers."

He slammed the door behind him.

"Are you all right?" said Raven as soon as she picked up the phone.

"Yeah, I'm okay. But the project isn't. We've got trouble. Big trouble."

"We've got some trouble here as well," she said.

He tensed. "What is it?"

"Your ex-wife is here."

"Janice?" Steele said. "She's *there*?"

"She's sitting right here on the couch. Security didn't want to let her up at first, but I told them it would be all right. They still scanned her and gave her a full body search. She wasn't very happy about it. And I don't think she's very happy about me, either."

"What's she doing there? What does she want?"

"You got me, lover. She won't tell me. Nice ladies like her don't talk to girls like me. But she seems very upset about something. She's been crying."

"Jesus. Her timing is fucking incredible. I'll be right over."

"All right, Doctor," Higgins said, once they were back in his office on the twenty-second floor. "You wanted to talk?"

"*Why*?" asked Dev. "Why was I kept out of the loop? Why wasn't I brought in on this?"

"The answer's very simple, Doctor," Higgins said. "You've become a security risk. I wasn't certain I could trust you."

Dev Cooper stared at him. "What the hell are you talking about?"

"Come on, who do you think you're talking to, Cooper?" Higgins said. "Did you really think you could keep secrets from me? Did you think I wouldn't find out about that program?"

"What program?"

Higgins rolled his eyes. "Please, spare me the innocent act, okay? I know all about that backup copy you've got of Steele's operating program. Gates made a copy for you, contrary to all regulations. I know that you've been working with it. You and Gates. And I know he wanted to tell me about it, but you blackmailed him into keeping quiet by threatening to report him for taking classified material home with him."

"You had my apartment bugged!"

"Of course I had your apartment bugged," said Higgins. "And with good reason, as it turns out. If it would safeguard the security of the government, I'd have a bug placed in every bedroom in this country. I ought to strip your clearance. By rights, I ought to have you thrown in jail. And I would, too, if I didn't need you right now."

"Jesus," Cooper said.

"Did you think we were playing *games* here, Doctor?" Higgins said. "Do you have any idea how much is at stake? What the hell did you think you were doing?"

"I wasn't committing treason, if that's what you're getting at," said Dev.

"Technically, that's exactly what you did," said Higgins. He held up his hand to forestall Cooper's reply. "Oh, I know you weren't thinking of selling that information or anything like that, but you've been doing some very peculiar things with that program. And I'd like very much to know what you've been up to."

"I wasn't 'up to' anything," said Cooper. "Look, you brought me out here to perform an almost impossible task. I was supposed to be the therapist to the first man in history who's ever received an artificial brain. Do you even have the slightest conception what a task like that entails? I was breaking entirely new ground in the field of psychiatry. There was no literature, no studies, absolutely nothing to guide me! I was groping in the dark like a blind man! When you first brought me out here from Los Alamos, you told me that I was going to be doing pioneering research in the field of psychocybernetics. You people were the ones who put Steele together.

I was the one who'd have to make sure his mind kept functioning normally. A computer mind, programmed with human mental engrams! Something like that has never even *existed* before!

"And I was expected to do my job with a patient who's got a natural antipathy toward psychiatrists, a patient I had only limited access to because you had him out on the streets, on the proving ground, as it were, getting you the right publicity you needed to get more funding from the legislature. I had nothing but an hour with him here, a half an hour with him there, whenever you or he felt it was convenient. How in the world did you expect me to conduct any kind of scientific observation under those circumstances?"

"So you decided to pull a copy of his backup program for yourself, so you could work with it at home," said Higgins.

"Gates gave me the idea," Cooper said. "He said that if I couldn't have access to Steele as much as I needed, there was no reason why I couldn't have the next best thing . . . a copy of the engram matrix he'd been programmed with. He said he could make a copy of the backup program for me, hook up a voice synthesizer peripheral programmed to sound just like Steele, and I'd be able to conduct my sessions with it at home. He said it would be the same as having Steele there, since it would be an exact copy of the data he'd been programmed with, and it would respond exactly as he'd respond. The only difference would be that I wouldn't have his body there, his actual physical self. He didn't seem to think it was necessary to go through all the red tape of requesting official clearance, since I already had triple-A clearance to work on the project and I was Steele's therapist."

"Are you seriously trying to tell me that you didn't realize you were violating security regulations?" Higgins said.

"Yes, yes, of course I knew," said Cooper, "but how could I possibly pass up such an opportunity? Don't you realize the implications? It could have opened up the door to a revolution in the science of psychotherapy! If you could download a patient's personality and make a backup copy, you'd be able to try out therapeutic techniques by working with the program and you'd know in advance how the patient would respond! It had the potential of completely eliminating the risk factor from psychotherapy! And you could dig deeper with a program, the way you'd never dare to do with the actual patient himself. I saw it as an opportunity not only to do my work with Steele, but also to try out the concept of computer surrogate therapy."

"And that's all you were doing?"

"Yes!"

"You didn't do anything to the program itself? To the backup copy that you pulled, I mean. You and Gates didn't modify it in any way?"

"No, of course not. Why would we?"

"Then why is it acting so strangely?"

"What do you mean?"

"I've got complete transcriptions of your sessions with the program, Doctor. It's responding in a very peculiar manner."

"So you know all about it then," said Dev.

"I heard what you said to Gates. Some sort of nonsense about its being self-aware, alive. You don't expect me to believe that?"

"It's true," said Dev. "It isn't nonsense. The program *is* self-aware. It *is* alive. You're making the same mistaken assumption that Gates made. You're thinking of it as merely another computer program, a sophisticated, artificial intelligence program, but that isn't what it is. Because he spent so much time working on debugging Steele's engram data, Gates allowed himself the conceit of thinking it was a program that he'd written. Only he *didn't* write it. All Gates really did was move information in the form of engram data from one place to another. The program isn't artificial intelligence, it's *real* intelligence, human mental engrams downloaded from a human brain and translated into software!

"What the hell do you think Steele *is*?" Cooper continued. "You think he's a machine? Yes, his brain is a computer, but it's programmed with data comprised of his own personality, his own identity. Do you think the backup program is different simply because it's a file in a computer, without a body? It's the same *exact* material that is contained in Steele's cybernetic brain! A backup copy of his very soul! Did you expect it to respond like a machine?"

Higgins frowned. "Gates said—"

"Gates was a brilliant man," said Dev, "but he was suffering from tunnel vision. A sort of tunnel vision that was entirely self-induced. Gates didn't want to believe that the program was self-aware because he didn't want to believe that *Steele* is self-aware. Not in any human sense, anyway."

"I don't understand," said Higgins. "You've lost me."

"Unlike you, Higgins," Dev said, "Gates was troubled with a little thing that's called a conscience. And to keep from being plagued by guilt, he devised an elaborate form of practicing denial. Gates convinced himself, with some purely technical justification, that Steele wasn't human because Steele had died. The moment brain function ceases, a man is considered legally dead. Gates used that rationale to convince himself that Steele had died the moment his organic brain was removed. Only his brain function never really ceased, did it? It was simply *moved* from one place to another. Gates chose not to think of it that way. The moment Steele's mental engrams were downloaded and translated into software, Gates chose to think of them as nothing more than a highly sophisticated AI program that he wrote. This gave him the luxury of seeing Steele as nothing more than a machine, a human body augmented with nysteel prosthetics and operated by cybernetics, but essentially a body from which the essence of humanity had flown. He deceived himself."

"Why would he do that?" asked Higgins, frowning.

"To avoid having to deal with the moral implications of what he'd done," said Cooper. "And to avoid the ethical implications inherent in having a backup copy of Steele's operating program."

"That was standard procedure," Higgins said. "We had to have a backup copy, in case anything happened to the original."

"Exactly," Cooper said. "Only it's one thing to make a backup copy of a computer program, but it's another thing entirely to duplicate a man's soul! And that's exactly what the backup copy of Steele's operating program is. A human personality reduced to software. A *duplicate* human personality. Christ, to you, it was just S.O.P. Make a backup copy. But you don't even realize what you've done, do you? You've xeroxed a human being! You've made an electronic clone!"

Higgins sat silent for a moment as it sank in. "I never thought of it that way," he said.

"Neither did Gates," said Cooper. "He didn't *want* to think of it that way. When I forced him to confront it, he didn't want to deal with it. It upset him terribly. I never should've rammed it down his throat that way. From a professional standpoint, it was unforgiveable, but I didn't have the time to handle Gates with kid gloves. I was worried about Steele, who's having a lot more trouble than you realize. And I was concerned about the program, because it's much more than just an ordinary computer program. It's a human identity. It thinks! It *feels*! It *lives*! I came out here to take care of one patient and now I've got two, one that's a cyborg and one that's engram data, *but they're both the same man*!"

"I see," said Higgins. "At least, I think I see. But why did you want to keep this from me? If Steele is having problems with his programming, we've got to go in and do something about it before the situation gets any worse."

Dev Cooper shook his head. "You still don't understand," he said.

"Then explain it to me."

"I knew there was something bothering Steele," Dev said. "I knew that he was keeping something from me, but I had no way of knowing what it was. At least, not until I got a backup copy of his program. I had Julie Nakamura show me how to install an imperative into the program . . . a set of commands that would require it to answer me, even if it didn't want to. You see, an ordinary computer program gives you whatever data you request from it, so long as it's contained within its files, because an ordinary computer program doesn't have free will. It can't *not want* to answer a question. But the engram matrix *has* free will, so it can refuse. What I needed was a sort of electronic equivalent of truth serum, and the imperative that Julie Nakamura wrote for me provided that."

"I see," said Higgins. "So the program had to tell you what was bothering it . . . what was bothering Steele . . . whether it wanted to or not?"

"Precisely," Cooper said. "There were bound to be certain inconsistencies between Steele's engram matrix and my backup copy, because since the time the matrix was loaded into Steele's brain, he's had certain experiences that the backup copy obviously hasn't had. However, I felt reasonably certain that whatever trouble Steele was having hadn't come about as a result of those experiences, but stemmed from something much more fundamental, something that was inherent in the matrix itself right from the beginning. You with me so far?"

"I think so. Go on."

"Well, despite the fact that it was under an imperative to answer me," said Dev, "it *still* resisted. Steele's got amazingly strong willpower. It was really quite unsettling. It was just like talking with a patient, only the patient had been booted up in my computer. And it wasn't easy. I was afraid of what might happen if the matrix discovered that it was only a backup copy. I wanted it to respond as if it were really Steele. And, in a sense, it really was . . . is . . . hell, even the semantics of the situation is difficult. Anyway, I allowed it to believe that it *was* Steele, the original Steele, that is, only it was on downtime, brought partially on line so that it could talk to me. I figured this would account for its not being aware of any feeling in its 'body.' And the matrix bought it. At first."

"What do you mean, at first?"

"I'll get to that. I started digging, trying to find out what was disturbing Steele. And, just as I'd suspected, it turned out to be related to the ancillary engram data Gates had originally used to supplement the matrix. Steele's been having nightmares. Dreams in which he's reliving experiences that he's never actually had. Only in another sense, he *has* had them, because they're now part of his memory. They've been programmed into him. As I tried explaining to Gates, the subconscious is an extremely complex thing. It isn't something you can treat as discrete data, it's more like a sort of thick, psychological soup, for lack of a better way of putting it. Gates was trained as a cybernetics engineer, not as a psychiatrist. He was used to thinking of things in mathematical terms, but you can't apply that kind of systemology to the subconscious. The operative word really *is* matrix. It's all blended together. You can't really isolate sections of it like bits of information in a computer program. It simply doesn't work that way.

"When Gates used ancillary engram data downloaded from other subjects to fill out Steele's program," Cooper continued, "he also wound up loading fragments of other people's subconsciouses into Steele's memory. These 'ghost personality fragments,' as I call them, are now expressing themselves through Steele's own subconscious. They've been blended into it. And, in his dreams, he's reliving bits and pieces of other people's lives, experiencing memories he can't account for. But he still feels like they're *his*, even though he knows they're not, because they've been blended into his matrix and they feel like a part of his identity. In effect, they are. The danger with that is that it might lead to his personality fragmenting."

"Then we're going to have to go in and erase them," Higgins said.

"That's just the point," said Dev. "You *can't*. That is, you probably can, but not without risking damage to Steele's identity. And he knows that. That's why he hasn't said anything about it. That's why he's kept it to himself. He's desperately trying to hang onto whatever he has left of his own identity. He's afraid to lose any part of himself. And if you tried to go into his matrix to erase the ghosts, it would be like trying to treat someone with an advanced case of lung cancer. You can't excise the cancer without also cutting out pieces of the lung. Steele is afraid that if we go in and try to debug his program and erase the ghosts, we'll also erase some very fundamental parts of him. He might not come out the same. And he's probably right."

"So what do we do?" asked Higgins.

"Not we, *me*," said Cooper. "This is what you brought me out here for. The only way to deal with this is to use conventional psychotherapy. Try to find a way to help him resolve this problem, to accept the ghosts and learn to live with them. Because otherwise, he might well wind up like Stalker, succumbing to electronic insanity."

"Great," said Higgins. "And I had to send him out to stop Stalker with all this going on inside him. The trouble is, I had no choice. Steele's all I've got. I haven't got the time to bring him in for extended therapy."

"You may not have to," Dev said. "Not if I can use the backup program to conduct some computer surrogate therapy and come up with a course of treatment. The problem is, it might not let me."

"What do you mean? Why not?"

"It's resisting the imperative," said Cooper. "It's very perceptive. It's got good instincts, Steele's instincts, and it's got a computer's capability of analyzing vocal response patterns. It analyzed mine and figured out that I was lying to it. It hasn't quite put it all together yet, but it now knows that it hasn't got a body. And it wants to know *why*."

3

Janice hadn't changed. She still looked as beautiful as ever. Her honey blond hair was worn long and loose to her shoulders, and her exquisite long legs were encased in tight jeans, the outfit completed with boots and a simple white blouse over which she wore a brown tweed sport jacket. Even in such casual, comfortable clothes, and despite the redness of her eyes from tears, she looked absolutely stunning, and Steele could not help being struck by the same old feelings.

There had always been an extremely strong chemistry between them, a powerful sexual attraction that they both had felt from the moment of their first meeting, when Shelley Taylor had introduced them. They slept together that first night, and Steele had fallen head over heels in love with her, but for Janice, it was never quite that simple. Steele was a cop on the Strike Force, and Janice didn't want anything to do with cops. Shelley's brother, Mick, was a Strike Force cop, and Janice had never gotten along with him very well. She detested what she saw as their swaggering braggadocio, their cock-of-the-walk demeanor and their "us versus them" attitude. She hated having to listen to their war stories. The world they lived in was a savage, violent world she didn't want to be exposed to. Steele wasn't like that. He didn't swagger as if he were some sort of modern gladiator. In social situations, he didn't dwell upon his exploits. He was soft-spoken and considerate, with a quiet strength about him that had appealed to her strongly. She was dismayed to find herself so powerfully attracted to him. From the very first, she'd wanted him and she knew he wanted her. It was like a hammer blow between the eyes. *Pow!* Chemistry.

She had gone to bed with him, but she was determined that it remain only a casual relationship. The last thing she wanted was to become seriously involved with a cop. In the kind of world they lived in, you never knew from one day to the next if he'd be coming home or if he was lying out there bleeding on a street somewhere. Janice didn't want that for herself. She didn't want that awful job coming home to her each night. But with the powerful attraction that they felt for one another, it was doomed not to remain a casual thing. Steele was serious right from the start, while she ran hot and cold. When he wasn't there, she kept telling herself she'd break it off, but when they were together, her desire for him overcame everything else and she just felt herself getting in deeper and deeper. When he proposed, her mind screamed no, but she said yes, and that ambivalence always remained to contaminate their marriage.

She wanted Steele the man, but she didn't want anything to do with Steele the cop. The trouble was, it was impossible to separate the two. Within a year, they had started to drift apart. Things got better for a while after Jason was born, with their new child occupying all their attention while they were home together, but it wasn't long before the downslide started once again. There was another respite with the birth of Cory, but children have never been enough to salvage a shaky marriage, and soon all the old tensions returned. In the bedroom, everything was great between them. Sexually, it was as if they were two precision-tooled parts of the same machine. But in ordinary, day-to-day life, they couldn't seem to get along.

Janice was never able to accept Steele's job, to accept the fact that it was more than just a job, that it was part and parcel of what and who he was, and she wound up resenting him. They stayed together for almost twenty years, largely because of the children, and because Steele was a Roman Catholic and a man who was very serious about the idea of commitment. But with every passing year, they became more and more distant. She felt trapped. They argued frequently, with Janice usually taking the slightest excuse to initiate a fight, and then they would make up in the bedroom, and she would apologize for "being such a bitch" and promise that things would get better, but they never got better. They only got worse.

Steele later discovered that at some point, she had started cheating on him with a succession of lovers. She didn't know he knew, and he had never wanted to find out the details, though Higgins had offered to supply them. For a long time, he blamed himself for not being able to fulfill her needs. Or even understand them. And he had only lately come to understand that, though perhaps he was not entirely innocent of blame in their disintegrating marriage, a large part of the responsibility for the failure of their relationship lay with Janice, who had listened to her crotch when it said yes and ignored her mind when it said no.

After he was ambushed by Borodini's soldiers and reconstructed as a cyborg, Janice had divorced him. She hadn't even bothered to wait to tell him to his face. It was all taken care of neatly and cleanly, while he was still undergoing the long series of operations, and when he came on line, the divorce was a *fait accompli*. Janice even left the city, leaving no forwarding address, and she had taken out a restraining order against him that prevented him from trying to see or contact her and the children. It was a restraining order that he could not contest, because the courts weren't anxious to decide the question of whether or not a computer had any civil rights. In her own words, she didn't want Jason and Cory to have "some kind of robot" for a father. He had not seen or heard from her or the children since. And now she was here, in his apartment, appearing out of nowhere, her eyes reddened with tears. The only reason Steele could think of for her coming back like this was that something had gone very badly wrong. He felt a knot forming in his stomach. He hoped the children were okay.

"Hello, Janice."

She looked up at him and managed a weak smile. Raven diplomatically left them alone together.

"Hello, Steele."

"You look good." He didn't know what else to say.

"So do . . . you," she said, somewhat uncertainly.

She had the look. The look he'd seen so many times before, when people found out what he was and stared at him with apprehension, with uncertainty, like looking at some alien creature, trying to discern a sign of the inhuman in the very human-looking man who stood before them.

"You mean I don't look like a robot, is that is?" he said, regretting it the moment he said it, but he couldn't help himself. It had always been that way with them. Too much history, too many years of pressure and frustration. They could never keep from sniping at each other. From sticking in the knife and giving it a little twist.

"I didn't say that," she said.

"You didn't have to. But then, you never really said anything, did you? You just decided to cut and run. You never even gave me the chance to say goodbye to the kids. You didn't even stick around long enough to say goodbye yourself. Is that all our relationship was worth?"

"I notice you didn't waste much time in finding yourself another one," she said. "She's very young, isn't she? Not what I would have thought of as your type. Where on earth did you find her? She looks like a hooker, for God's sake."

"Maybe that's because she was a hooker," Steele said.

She starred at him. "You're kidding."

"No. But the operative word is *was*."

"You surprise me," she said. "I wouldn't have thought that you could sink so low."

"It's not your place to judge either me or Raven," Steele said tensely, determined to hold his temper in check. "At least since she's been with me, she hasn't slept around. Which is a lot more than I could say for you."

She grimaced. "So you knew. What did you do, hire a detective?"

Steele sighed. "Forget it, Janice. All that's ancient history.

It doesn't matter now. What matters is the present. What are you doing here? What do you want? Is it the kids? Is something wrong?"

She nodded and started to cry again.

"What is it?" he said, concerned.

"It's Cory," she said, blinking back tears. "She's run away from home. And . . . and I don't know where Jason is. He's gone to look for her. We had a fight. An awful fight . . . I . . . thought they might be with you."

"I haven't seen them," Steele said with concern.

"Would you tell me if you had?"

"What are you saying, Janice? You think I'd try to take them from you?"

"The thought occurred to me."

Steele shook his head. "After all those years, I thought you knew me better than that."

"I don't know you *now*," she said defensively. "I don't . . . I just don't know you anymore, Steele. I don't know who you are. Or even . . . what you are."

He let that pass. There was no point in arguing with her, no point in trying to convince her of anything.

"Did you go to the police?"

"Yes. I filed a missing persons report. But they told me there really wasn't much that they could do. There are so many runaways. . . . I told them about you. They said they would investigate, but. . . ."

"I haven't heard anything yet. What police department was it?"

She hesitated.

"Come on, Janice, for God's sake. If I wanted to, I could have found out where you lived at any time in less than five minutes, just by picking up a phone."

"Boston," she said.

"What made you think Cory might've come here?" he said.

"She left a note. She said something about going home. I thought she meant you."

"I haven't seen or heard from Cory and Jason since you took them away," he said.

She broke down and started sobbing.

Steele put his arms around her as she sobbed into his chest. "Okay, okay," he said. "Try to calm down. Tell me what happened."

"I . . . I told them you were dead," she said, looking away guiltily. "That you'd been killed. All right, it was a stupid thing to do, I know, but . . . at the time . . . I mean, I had to tell them *something*. I couldn't tell them that their father had become a. . . ." her voice trailed off.

"A machine?" said Steele.

"They were children!" she said. "How the hell do you explain something like that to *children*?"

"You tell them the truth," he said. "They're teenagers. They're certainly old enough to understand about a thing like divorce. I think they might have understood the rest of it as well, if you only gave them half a chance. You had no right doing what you did, Janice. Regardless of what you think of me, regardless of what you think I am, I'm still their father. If nothing else, they had a right to know the truth. Did you really think they wouldn't find out?"

"I . . . I don't know what I thought," she said miserably. "I was confused. I was frightened. I was . . ."

"All right, never mind all that. Go on."

"They found out about you. I couldn't keep it from them. It was all over the news, on television. . . . We had a terrible fight. They said awful things to me, horrible things. . . ."

"Can you really blame them?"

"Damn you, Steele, I was only trying to do what I thought was best for them!"

"No, you weren't. You were trying to do what you thought was best for you. All right, forget it. I'm sorry I said that. The important thing now is to find them. When did Cory run away?"

"Five days ago. And Jason the day after. I was sure they were with you. I thought the police would come and get them and bring them back! And I . . . I just couldn't bring myself to call you and . . . and . . . I waited as long as I could, but when I didn't hear anything. . . ."

"Jesus Christ," said Steele.

"Where are they, Steele? *Tell me*! You've got no right to keep my children from me!"

"I haven't got them, Janice. I don't have the faintest idea where they are. This is the first I've heard of this, I swear to you."

"I don't believe you! You're lying!"

"I don't know where they are, Janice, but I promise you, I'll do everything I can to find them."

"You mean you *really* haven't got them? Oh, my God. Oh, my God. . . ."

"Take it easy. I'll get the police here working on it right away. I'll put word out on the streets, and I'll have someone call Boston and see if we can't light a fire under them, just in case they haven't left the city. Meanwhile, the best thing you can do is to go home. There's nothing you can do here. Go back to Boston and as soon as I hear anything, I'll let you know."

"You promise?"

"I promise. Look, for all we know, they might even come back on their own. You certainly won't be doing them any good here."

"I suppose you're right. I've just been frantic . . . I thought . . . if anything happens to them. . . ."

"I'll find them, Janice. I promise you, I'll find them. Now go home and let me get to work on it. And if they come back, let me know at once. Don't worry, I won't try to interfere. Your restraining order is still in effect."

She looked up at him, her eyes brimming with tears. "I'm sorry," she said. "It's just that I. . . ." She shook her head. "Can't you try to understand?"

"I can try. But that isn't important now. The important thing is to find Cory and Jason and make sure they're all right."

She looked down at the floor and nodded. He walked her to the door. Then he turned to see Raven standing in the doorway of their bedroom.

"I heard," she said. "Are you all right?"

"No," he said softly. "No, I'm not all right. I've got to find a psychopathic cyborg who's loose somewhere in the city, a man who used to be my partner and my friend. And now my kids are out there somewhere, too, and I promised her I'd find them. But if they don't show up here, I really don't know what I can do."

"There's some people I can talk to," she said. "And Ice can help. We can put the word out, find out if anybody's seen them. It's a long shot, but you never know. Chances are they might even show up here. Have you got any pictures of them?"

Steele nodded. "Yeah. I'll get some copies made when I file a report down at Strike Force headquarters. I've got to go down there anyway and take charge of the Stalker operation." He sighed heavily. "I've got to go put together a manhunt to find my best friend and kill him."

Officer Manny Esteban and his partner, Sergeant Harry Crane, were cruising in their radio motor patrol car near the edge of Midtown, on west 34th Street, when a man stepped out onto the street right in front of them. Crane had to slam on the brakes to keep from hitting him.

"Jesus fucking Christ!" he swore. "Did you see that? Stupid son of a bitch almost got himself—"

He didn't get any farther. The man bent over, grasped the bumper of their vehicle and, to their utter disbelief, lifted the front wheels right up into the air. Before they could react, he threw the patrol car over on its side. The roof buckled as it rolled over, crushing the lights and siren.

"*Holy shit!*" cried Crane as they were thrown out of their seats and against each other.

He awkwardly clawed for his holster, but before he could get the gun out, their attacker ripped the driver's side door off its hinges and threw it in the street behind him. He reached in, grabbed Crane and dragged him out. As Esteban struggled to open the door and get out on his side, Stalker lifted Crane up into the air as if he were a doll, swung him around and smashed his head against the upturned car with brutal force, snapping his neck and breaking his skull open like an egg. Esteban finally got the door open and scrambled out on his side of the car. He rolled to his feet and pulled his gun out. He fired across the exposed undercarriage of the car three times. All three bullets struck Stalker squarely in the chest. They didn't even slow him down.

Gaping in astonishment, Esteban squeezed off another three shots as the assailant came around the car, heading for him. Esteban kept firing until he emptied the whole clip, with no apparent effect. Several of the shots struck the copkiller in the head, but aside from having his neck snapped back briefly by the impact of the 9mm. hollowpoints, the bullets seemed completely ineffective.

Stalker reached out and plucked the gun from Esteban's grasp. He squeezed it in his right hand and crushed it. Solid steel. Crumpled it as if it were nothing more than paper. He tossed it aside and grabbed Esteban by the shoulders. Esteban screamed as the powerful hands squeezed, and there was a sharp, crackling sound as the bones in his upper arms splintered. He felt himself being bent back against the upturned car, his spine strained to the breaking point as his assailant brought his face up close to his.

"I want Steele," he said hoarsely. "You understand? You *hear* me?"

Esteban cried out in agony.

"It's his fault they did this to me," Stalker said. "It's his fault and I'm going to make him pay. I'm going to kill him for what he made them do to me. Him and every goddamn cop in this lousy, motherfucking city. Every one of them is gonna pay. Every single one."

Esteban was abruptly released. He sank down to the street, unable to support himself with his arms. He waited for the killing blow, but it didn't come. When he looked up, Stalker was gone. Whimpering with pain, his arms hanging limp and useless at his sides, Esteban crawled like a worm back inside the overturned patrol car. He tried not to look at his partner's corpse lying in the street, its head broken open like a melon. Using his teeth, he managed to get the handset off its hook and radio in a call for help.

Jacob Hardesty was a big, ham-fisted, gravel-voiced, bull of a
man, the chief of the NYPD's Special Operations Division,
more commonly known as the Strike Force. He and Steele
went back together a long way. He had been Steele's training
officer when Steele was just a rookie, and later on, he had been
Steele's sergeant. When Steele made sergeant, Jake "Hardass"
Hardesty was his lieutenant and now he was the chief, getting
old and heavy behind his massive, burn-scarred and coffee-
stained desk, a good street-cop stuck in the bureaucratic limbo
between the commissioner's and mayor's offices and the men
under his command. And as if he didn't have enough trouble,
now he'd have to clean up a mess made by the feds and
somehow manage to do it without telling the media a thing.

"I'd just gotten off the phone with your man, Higgins, when
the call came in," he said to Steele. "We've got two officers
down. One dead, one seriously wounded. According to the
surviving officer, Patrolman Esteban, Stalker stepped out in
front of their RMP and flipped it over like it was a toy. Then
he ripped off the door, pulled out Sergeant Crane and bashed
his brains out. Esteban said he emptied an entire clip into him,
chest *and* head, and Stalker just kept right on coming. He
disarmed Esteban and pulverized the bones in both his shoulders. And while he was at it, he mentioned *your* name."

"My name?" Steele said.

"Yeah," said Hardesty. "Esteban was in shock, but he was
very definite on that point. Apparently, Stalker seems to feel
that you're responsible for what's happened to him. And he
intends to kill you. You and every other police officer in the
city."

"Christ," said Steele.

"Stopping him is going to be a problem in itself," said
Hardesty. "What I'd like to know is how the hell am I supposed
to do it *and* keep the media from finding out about it? Higgins
seemed to think that—"

"Screw Higgins," Steele said. "Higgins put me in charge of
this operation. If the media starts bugging you for a statement,

then *give* them one. Tell 'em the whole story. And if Higgins gives you any shit about it, refer him straight to me."

"You sure about this?" Hardesty said. "Higgins seems determined to keep this whole thing under wraps. If I blow the story and then tell him I had your authorization, it'll all come down on you."

"So?" said Steele. "What are they going to do? Pull my plug? They *need* me, Jake. Right now, I'm all they've got. Hell, all Higgins is interested in doing is covering his ass. Only I'm not going to let him do that at the expense of the people of this city. Besides, I don't see how he can. This whole thing is going to blow up right in his face. I'd rather the people had the right information up front than fuel media speculation with all sorts of stupid denials. We're going to have enough trouble on our hands."

"Which brings us back to the main problem," Hardesty said. "How are we going to stop this guy? If I understood correctly, he's got everything you've got and then some. We haven't even got a proper make on him yet. Esteban gave us a description, but there's been no time to get a composite sketch made up—"

"You can do better than that," said Steele. "You've got his photograph."

"We do?" said Hardesty.

"He used to be a Strike Force cop," said Steele. "Pull the files on Mick Taylor."

Hardesty's jaw dropped open. *"Mick Taylor?"* he said with disbelief. "But I thought he was dead! I went to his funeral, for Christ's sake!"

"You didn't see a body, did you?"

"No. There was no body. They said he'd been—"

"They lied," said Steele. "They lied to Shelley, they lied to me, they lied to you and all Mick's friends. They've had Mick on ice ever since we were ambushed together in Harlem. They kept him on life support until they got the funding to build themselves another cyborg. I worked out so well, the Finance Committee okayed their new budget and they went ahead with a brand new and improved model, designated Stalker. A prototype for a new generation police and military cyborg.

Superior construction. Laser and plasma weapons systems.
And I don't know what the hell else. It seems the engineers
threw in a whole bunch of improvements, just to show off what
they could do given enough money. Only now no one can tell
us exactly what they did, because they're all dead and Stalker
smashed their data banks when he ran amok in the lab
complex."

"Jesus," Hardesty said, letting his breath out in a heavy
sigh. "Laser and plasma weapons systems?" He shook his
head. "I'm not even sure I *want* to know what else he may
have. And on top of that, it's Mick, as if things weren't bad
enough. Mick Taylor had a lot of friends in this department."

"I know, Jake. He was my partner," Steele said. He walked
over to the window in Hardesty's office and stared out through
the grimy glass. "But that's not Mick Taylor out there," he said
quietly. "Maybe it was Mick once, but not anymore. I don't
know what they did to him. Maybe something went wrong with
his cybernetic brain. Maybe the software was bad; hell, I don't
know. But whatever it was, Mick Taylor's gone now. What
we've got out there is some kind of Frankenstein's monster. A
criminally insane computer brain in a superhuman body. And
the kindest thing that we could do to it is put it out of its
misery." He turned to look at Hardesty. "It's what I'd want for
myself, if it ever happened to me."

Hardesty met his gaze, and to his credit, he didn't look away
when he asked, "You think there's any chance of that?"

Steele compressed his lips in a tight grimace. "I honestly
don't know, Jake." He shook his head and sighed. "No, that's
a cop-out. There's a chance. It happened to him, so I guess that
means it could happen to me, too. And if it did, I'd want the
job done quickly and efficiently. We owe Mick at least that
much."

"Okay," said Hardesty. "How do you want to play it?"

"We'll issue a city-wide all points," said Steele. "All units.
Have all the watch commanders pass out photos of Mick with
strict instructions that if any RMP encounters him, they are to
avoid contact *at all costs* and immediately get on the horn to
Strike Force. Stress that. We don't want any heros, Jake. Look

what happened to Esteban and Crane. Regular RMP units just don't have the ordnance to deal with Stalker. If he tries to engage any of them, their orders are to run."

"*Run*?" said Hardesty.

"That's right," said Steele. "Run like hell. Or Stalker will take them apart. We're going to need well-trained Strike Force personnel and some serious ordnance to take him out. Higgins is going to have several squads of federal troops standing by to back us up, so we'll have to set up a comlink between our people on the streets, headquarters and the Federal Building. We'll organize the entire division into flying squads, each man equipped with full riot gear, magazines loaded with high explosive and armor-piercing ammo. The squads will work standard duty rotation, with the federal squads on stand-by. That way, we can have people out covering the city as much as possible, with the feds in reserve for a fast chopper drop the minute we get a contact. We'll need as many choppers in the air as we can spare, both scouting for Stalker and ready to pick up and transport squads across the city at a moment's notice. Higgins can loan us a few choppers as well."

"You want one for yourself?"

"I've already requisitioned one from the agency. A small X-wing. They're faster."

"Okay," said Hardesty. "Anything else?"

Steele paused. "Yeah," he said. "One more thing. Something personal. I just saw Janice."

"Janice?" Hardesty said, surprised. "She's back in town?" Then he frowned. "What's wrong?"

"The kids are missing," Steele said. "Cory ran away from home and Jason apparently took off to look for her."

"Oh, hell," said Hardesty.

"Janice thought they might've come down here to see me, but there's been no sign of them. She filed a report in Boston, that's where they're living now, but it seems they haven't really done anything about it. You know how it is with runaways. They're not a high priority. I thought maybe you could do me a favor and give the Boston PD a call, ask them to take a little extra trouble. And circulate some photos of the kids around our own department, just in case. I brought some along."

"Of course," said Hardesty, reaching for the photos. "I'll get these duped and put the word out immediately. Let our people know it's family."

"Thanks, Jake. I appreciate it."

"Don't mention it. It's a hell of a time for something like this, ain't it?"

"Yeah," said Steele with a tight grimace.

"Maybe they'll show up at your place."

"I hope so, Jake," said Steele. "I sure as hell hope so."

They lived down in the subway tunnels. It was dark and comforting down there, like a vast womb of steel and concrete. A few of the tunnels, where several trains still ran beneath the streets of Midtown, were illuminated every few yards by worklights, but they generally avoided those. They kept to the tunnels that were abandoned and falling into disrepair, plunged into stygian darkness.

It was cold and damp down in the tunnels, but in the winter, it was warmer than the streets above and safer than the abandoned, crumbling ruins that dotted no-man's-land. There they would have had to worry about the gangs that controlled their turf with an iron hand. The gangs would have taken a dim view of predators like them. Here, down in the tunnels, they could hide. And hunt.

Many of them no longer remembered what their names were. They had become mere shadows of human beings, wraith-like entities that shambled through the underground tunnels like specters. They dressed in layers of smelly rags and cast-off clothes, whatever they could find. Or take from their victims. Their hair was long, matted and scraggly, falling to their shoulders like Spanish moss. Their faces were gaunt and craggy, deeply etched with lines that were filled in with dirt and grime. Their eyes were deeply sunken, their vision preternaturally acute in almost total darkness. They looked emaciated, but their appearance was deceptive. They were far from harmless. And the women were just as savage as the men.

They looked just like what they were . . . ghouls. Cadaverous feasters of human flesh. It was only fitting that they live underground.

They hunted together like packs of starving wolves, lurking near the gateways to the surface in anticipation of unwary and uncautious prey. Work crews tried to keep the old subway entrances sealed, but it was a losing battle. The tunnel dwellers always broke through once again or found other ways up out of their warren. From time to time, the Strike Force cops descended into the tunnels in attempts to clean them out, but it was a task akin to trying to eradicate the city's rats and roaches. There were always more of them and there were too many places where they could hide from the exterminators.

Often, driven by madness and starvation, they fought amongst themselves like rabid dogs and ate the flesh of those they killed. Unlike the raving screamers, they were not totally devoid of reason. Though many of them were mentally deranged, not a few were sane . . . if killing and eating their own kind could, by any stretch of the imagination, possibly be considered sane. But in a world such as the one they lived in, normal definitions did not often apply. Normality did not apply. It would be closer to the truth to say that they were rational as opposed to sane. They knew full well what they were doing. Unlike some of the more disturbed among them, most were fully in touch with reality. They found ways to rationalize what they had become. They blamed circumstances and society. They told themselves and one another that they had no choice, that they were driven to hunt and consume their own kind by a desperate imperative of survival, because the world above cared nothing for them. And, in that, at least, they were not entirely wrong.

A group of them was sitting around a fire they had built on the rusted tracks where two tunnels intersected. They huddled close to the flames. Their faces, illuminated in the flickering firelight, were the faces of the lost, visions from some surrealistic painting by Doré or Bosch, the faces of the damned. Some of their eyes were empty, staring vacantly into the dancing flames. Others glinted with the light of madness.

It had been a long time since they had eaten, and at such times, the group dynamic became a very tenuous thing. The tension was palpable among them. They were hungry. They were tired. And each of them was wondering who would be the first to fall asleep.

The sound of approaching footsteps galvanized them. Like animals, their ears pricked up. They listened. There was only one pair of footsteps. One individual approaching. They exchanged quick and hungry glances. Not a threat. A victim.

Or so they thought.

As the footsteps drew nearer, echoing throughout the tunnel, they scuttled back into the shadows, away from the firelight. They drew back into the niches in the tunnels, put there so that track workman could get back out of the way of passing subway trains. They waited, fingering their weapons, carving knives and fire axes, clubs with nails driven into them, sharpened sticks of wood, iron pipes, steel concrete reinforcing rods, whatever they could find and use to kill their prey. The footsteps stopped.

The dark figure of a man stood just beyond the firelight, in the center of the tunnel. Perhaps he'd be attracted by the fire's warmth. Perhaps he'd be too afraid to risk coming any closer. No matter. If he fled, they'd run him down. He was a big man, but they'd bring him down by the sheer weight of their numbers. And his size meant that there would be enough to go around for all of them to have their fill.

He simply stood there, waiting. They licked their lips in hungry anticipation. Why didn't he come closer? Why didn't he run? Why didn't he *do* something?

They weren't aware that he knew exactly where they were. They didn't know that he could hear them breathing, that with his cybernetically enhanced senses, he could even hear their hearts beating. That he could see even better than they could in the dark.

A few could wait no longer. They stepped out of their hiding places, holding their makeshift weapons in their hands. More of them came out. Slowly, they approached him, watching, waiting for him to bolt in fear.

Only he didn't bolt. He simply stood there, watching them. And waiting.

A few of them were almost within reach of him. *Why didn't he run?* Perhaps his mind was too far gone. They hesitated. What if he was a screamer? But no, screamers didn't act that way. Screamers were like howling beasts, wailing themselves hoarse and clawing at their agonizing wounds, their minds completely gone, attacking anything that moved. Like the predatory creatures that they were, the tunnel dwellers tried to sense his fear, the emotion that would galvanize them into action, but there was something wrong. They could not tell what it was. This man was not afraid. Somehow, they knew this man was dangerous.

Slowly, they drew closer, moving around the fire on either side.

And then, just as they were about to spring, their quarry's eyes suddenly lit up with two bright, glowing pinpoints of red light.

They froze, eyes wide, mouths open, staring at the large, shadowy figure with the hellfire in his eyes.

He raised his arm and white heat seemed to belch forth from his outstretched fingers. The plasma burst struck the fire behind them and blossomed into a huge flower of flame, shooting sparks and burning cinders throughout the tunnel. As they cried out and started to fall back in terror, Stalker fired again, the plasma flame blocking their escape.

"Freeze," he said. "Stand where you are or burn."

There was nowhere to run. They stood before him, helpless, quaking with fear. Several of them soiled themselves.

"Follow me and I'll get you food and weapons," he said. "Guns and ammunition. Do as I say and I'll let you live."

"Who . . . who are you?" one of them said in a trembling voice. "*What* are you?"

"Your death," he said. "Or your life. The choice is yours. It doesn't matter to me, one way or the other. So what's it going to be?"

They stood there, terrified, instinctively huddling closer to one another.

"You said . . . you could get us food?" said one of them. "Meat? *Fresh* meat?"

"And weapons," he said. "Guns. Enough for all of you. Only if you try to use them against me, I'll kill you. Like this."

He raised his other arm and a bright beam of collimated laser light suddenly lanced out from it, striking one of the tunnel dwellers right between the eyes. He cried out briefly and crumpled to the ground.

"Don't! Don't kill us! *Please*! We'll do anything you say! *Anything*!"

Stalker smiled. "I thought you would."

4

The call from Raven came during Steele's briefing to the officers of Strike Force. When the desk sergeant found out what it was about, he called Captain Hardesty at once. Jake left the briefing and took the call. When Steele came out of the briefing room, Hardesty was waiting for him.

"Go home," he said. "It's your son. He's there with Raven. She says someone really worked him over."

Officer Kev Bishop was right behind Steele as they were coming out of the briefing room, and he immediately said, "Come on, we'll take my unit."

They drove at top speed back to Steele's building. As they pulled up to the curb, Bishop said, "Want me to wait?"

"No, get back to your squad. I've got a chopper standing by up on the pad," said Steele. "And Kevin . . . thanks."

"Don't mention it."

Steele hurried to the elevator and took it up to the penthouse floor. As he came in, Raven was coming out of the guest room with another man. He was carrying a medical bag.

"Lt. Steele?" he said. "I'm Dr. Courtney. Security took the liberty of calling me. I'm on staff at the Federal Building."

"How bad is he?" said Steele.

"He'll be all right," said Dr. Courtney, reassuring him. "It looks much worse than it really is. He was beaten up, but

51

outside of a broken nose, some lacerations and contusions, he doesn't seem to have been seriously injured. Whoever hit him was apparently wearing some heavy rings, which accounts for the cuts. I was concerned about possible fractures and internal bleeding, but there seems to be no sign of that. I'd like to have him in for X-rays, just to make sure, but the important thing right now is for him to get some rest. Aside from his injuries, he was quite distraught. I'd say he's been under a great deal of stress recently. I've just given him a sedative. He should remain in bed for a few days. Here's my card; call me if there's any change, but I think he'll be all right. I'll have my office set up an appointment for him to come in in a couple of days, but I don't think there's any need for hospitalization. At the very worst, I think we may be looking at some hairline fractures, but outside of his nose, nothing has been broken."

"Can I see him? Is he awake?"

"He should be getting a bit groggy by now, but yes, by all means, go and see him. He's been asking for you."

"Thank you, Doctor. I really appreciate your coming."

"No trouble at all. And don't worry about my bill, it's been taken care of by the agency."

"Thanks just the same."

Steele went in to see his son.

"Dad . . . ?"

Steele felt a lump in his throat. His stomach knotted up. Both because he hadn't seen his son in such a long time and because he was now seeing him like this. In his time as a Strike Force cop, he had seen much worse, far, far worse, but this was his own son. Jason lay in bed, on his back. His broken nose was taped. The blood had been cleaned off, and the doctor had said it wasn't serious, but Jason had been thoroughly worked over. One eye was puffed almost completely shut. His mouth was cut. The rings on the hands of whoever'd beat him up had severely lacerated his face. He was a mass of bruises, all black and blue and swollen.

"Jason . . ."

He came over to the bed, kneeled and took the boy in his arms. If he could have wept, he would have, but bionic eyes don't cry. Jason's arms tried to go around him, but he was already succumbing to the sedative. His voice was thick and slurred, partly from the drug and partly from the swelling and the damage to his lips.

"Mom said . . . you were dead. . . . She told us . . ."

"We can talk about that later," Steele said. "Who did this to you?"

"I'm . . . sorry, Dad. . . ."

"*Sorry*? Sorry for what, for God's sake? What happened? Tell me."

"Feel tired . . . sleepy . . . beat me up . . ."

"*Who* beat you up?"

"Pim . . ."

"Tim? Tim who?"

"No . . . not Tim . . . Pim . . . mmmpf . . ."

"Jason?"

"Let him sleep, Steele," Raven said from the doorway. "He's been through a real bad time."

Jason's eyes flickered and then closed. In seconds, he was breathing deeply. Steele leaned forward and kissed his son on the forehead. He rose to his feet and left the room, shutting the door softly behind him.

"Did he tell you what happened?" he said.

Raven lit a cigarette. Her hand wasn't steady.

"Yes. He told me," she said flatly.

"*Well*?"

Raven inhaled the smoke deeply and then let it out in a long exhalation. "You better sit down," she said.

Seeing the expression on her face, Steele said nothing. He moistened his lips nervously and sat down on the couch.

"Go ahead," he said.

"He was beaten up by a pimp," she said.

"A *pimp*? Are you saying he had some trouble with a hooker?"

"Not with a hooker," Raven said. "*Because* of a hooker." She took a deep breath and shook her head. "There just isn't any easy way to say this. Your daughter's been turned out."

Steele stared at her.

She held his gaze.

"What are you saying?"

"Cory's pimp beat him up."

"No." He shook his head. "No. There must be some mistake. You didn't hear him right, you—"

"We had a chance to talk before the doctor came," she said. She came over and sat down beside him. "I don't know how it happened, but I think I can guess. I've seen it many times before. She came to town, alone and frightened, thinking she'd burned all her bridges, too scared to go back home. You're not in the phone book. She didn't know where you were living now, maybe that didn't even occur to her when she left, and she probably thought if she went to the police they'd pick her up and hold her while they called her mother. . . . She was scared and lost, she hadn't really thought it through, and a kind stranger came up and started talking to her. Asked her if she was all right, if she was in trouble, maybe he could help, buy her a cup of coffee, talk about it—"

"No," said Steele, numbly, shaking his head. "No . . ."

"She had a friend. A girl named Marcia?"

Steele looked at her. "Marcia Kastner. Her best friend. Her family lived in the same building. The two of them went to school together."

Raven nodded. "Jason thought Cory might have gone to see her. He said they were very close. Well, Marcia had seen Cory. Cory called her. They met on 110th Street, near the park. Cory was crying. She said she was in trouble. She asked her to call Jason, to say she needed help. She told her . . ." Raven sighed and looked away. "Damn it, Steele, I'm sorry."

Steele felt as if he'd been punched in the stomach.

"Oh, God . . ." he said.

"She didn't know where you were," said Raven. "And she was afraid to call the cops and ask for help. And probably, she was ashamed."

Steele winced and shut his eyes. "She's only fifteen. She's just a little girl. Oh, Christ. Oh, Jesus Christ . . ."

Raven put her arms around him. For a long moment, they

simply sat there, holding each other, then Steele pulled himself together and took a deep breath.

"All right," swallowing hard. "Tell me the rest of it."

"Marcia tried to call Jason up in Boston, but he'd already left to look for Cory. And Cory made her promise not to tell anybody else. Only Jason. Your ex-wife hit her with a lot of questions, and Marcia just hung up on her. She didn't know what to do. Then Jason showed up, and she told him the whole story. Cory had called her several times, and the next time she called, Marcia gave her Jason's number. He had some money in a savings account that he'd withdrawn when he left, and he was staying in some fleabag hotel. Cory wouldn't give him her number. She was afraid. They agreed to meet at the same place where Cory had met Marcia, by the park, only her pimp became suspicious and he followed her. Jason tried to take him on and the bastard beat him up, with Cory standing there and watching. And while Jason was lying there and bleeding, he told her if she ever tried to get in touch with him again, he'd kill him."

"Who was he?" Steele said, his voice hard. "What's the bastard's name?"

Raven shook her head. "Jason didn't know. Cory never told him. But he said he could identify him."

Steele reached for the phone and dialed Strike Force.

"This is Steele," he said. "Let me talk to the old man. Right now."

A moment later, Jake came on the line.

"Steele . . . I was just about to call you, we—"

"Jake, I want somebody down here with pictures of every single pimp that the department's got on file, and I want it done yesterday. Get—"

"Steele, listen to me, I don't know what this is all about, but it's gonna have to wait. Get on that chopper right away. Stalker's just been sighted down at Grand and Orchard. We've got units moving in."

"*Damn it*!" Steele said. "Jake, stay on the line. I'm on my way." He gave the phone to Raven. "Tell Hardesty what happened. Stalker's just been sighted. I've gotta move."

"I'll take care of it," she said.

Feeling torn, Steele ran to the arms cabinet, grabbed his assault rifle, scooped up some magazines and ran out to the helipad, where the small X-wing was standing by. The pilot was having a smoke in the cockpit. The moment he saw Steele coming, he tossed the cigarette out and started up the engines. Steele leaped into the cockpit.

"Lower East Side, Grand and Orchard," he shouted. "*Move it!*"

The X-wing rose up into the air, banking steeply.

Steele quickly checked his weapons. His son had been beaten to a pulp, and somewhere out there, his fifteen-year-old daughter was turning tricks for a sadistic pimp, and there was nothing he could do to help her. He wished he could have told Jake to go to hell. And Higgins, too, and all the rest of them. But there was no way he could do that. The knowledge that Cory had been turned into a hooker twisted in his gut like a knife.

He remembered what it had been like when he had first met Raven, whose crime-boss boyfriend had dumped her on a pimp in no-man's-land. She had been gang-raped by a dozen men, members of a savage street gang called the Skulls. The thought of Cory going through such an ordeal was more than he could bear. But until Jason came around again and could identify the pimp, there was nothing he could do. And Stalker was a deadly threat, a mad killer who could not be ignored.

His son lay back in the apartment, his handsome young face a symphony of cuts and bruises; his daughter forced into prostitution and his best friend turned into a psychotic killing machine. Ever since he had awakened from his coma to discover that he had become a cyborg, part man and part machine, Steele had held on with desperation to the human part of himself, telling himself that he was not a robot, that he had not lost his soul, that he was more than just a computer encased in flesh and blood.

The complex cybernetic matrix that was his mental engram programming left him with all his memories and all his feelings intact, but for once, for the first time since it happened, he found himself wishing that he *was* merely a machine, that he could turn off his emotions. But he couldn't. And they raged within him like a firestorm. He felt powerless. Completely helpless. And consumed with hate. Hate for the whole world. Hate for the savage urban jungle that had done this to him and to his family. And he thought that he could begin to understand the rage that fueled the renegade cyborg that was once Mick Taylor, his former partner and best friend. A man whom he had worked with, a man who had been closer to him than his wife, a man whom he had loved . . . and whom he would now have to kill.

If he could.

Dev Cooper had been the picture of robust and virile health when he had first arrived at Project Steele headquarters from Los Alamos. A lanky Texan, fit and tanned from the southwestern sun. It hadn't been all that long ago. Project Steele had changed him. He had lost weight. He was pale. He slept poorly, when he slept at all, and there were deep bags under his eyes. Often, he forgot to shave. His easygoing demeanor had been replaced by a frenetic nervousness. He had started smoking and he lit one cigarette after another, always needing to have something in his hands, always fidgeting.

His only previous vice had been drinking a bit too much, but now he drank incessantly. In the morning, some hair of the dog to steady his nerves. At work, he kept a bottle in his desk and he poured booze into his coffee thermos. He drank throughout the day and then he drank some more at night. He was one of those rare drunks who did not act drunk, unless one looked very closely and saw that something was just a bit off kilter with his eyes. Drinking slowed his reflexes, but he handled it well enough that it did not interfere with his work—at least he told himself it didn't—and it never affected his speech. If anything, it slowed him down to a more normal mode, because his perpetual high-strung state gave him the metabolism of a high-performance dragster. But he knew that it could not continue. If he was not already an alcoholic, he was well on his way to becoming one.

But he needed it. He needed the booze and pills, those time-honored crutches of psychiatrists who had shouldered too heavy an emotional burden and were heading straight for burnout. He recalled the hoary old joke among his colleagues, the story of a young psychiatrist, fresh from his residency, opening a private practice. At the end of his first week, the young doctor is a wreck, emotionally drained. He gets into the elevator after closing up his office and, on the way down, the elevator stops at a lower floor and another psychiatrist gets on, a respected older doctor whose name is well known among his peers. He asks the younger doctor how he's doing, and the younger man breaks down, cataloging all the stress and pain he's been exposed to, asking the older doctor how he can possibly stand it, listening to it day-in and day-out. And the older doctor simply shrugs and says, "Who listens?"

Well, there was one patient in particular that Cooper had to listen to, was compelled to listen to, and that patient frightened him more than any other patient he had ever had in his entire career. He had specialized in abnormal psychology, often treating people who were truly far gone around the bend, split personalities and schizophrenics, some of them extremely dangerous. But this patient was the most dangerous of all. And though Dev Cooper did not feel any physical threat from this patient, he felt a threat to his immortal soul.

The patient's name was Steele. Not Donovan Steele, cyborg, but Donovan Steele, program. A backup copy of the mental engram matrix that Steele had been programmed with. An electronic clone. A program that was alive and self-aware. A program that had just discovered what it was.

For most of his adult life, Dev Cooper had not believed in God. He had thought of himself more as an agnostic rather than an atheist, because it seemed to him that atheists made a religion of their non-belief, and as a scientist, Dev Cooper could not take refuge in that kind of certainty. Atheism, in itself, was just as much an act of faith as any other religion. Dev Cooper had not believed in God because he had not thought there was one, at least not as He was painted on the canvas of the Judeo-Christian tradition. If there was some "guiding intelligence" behind the creation of all things, Dev did not believe that it was anything that could be personified in human terms, something that cared about humanity in individual or even general terms, something that could be petitioned by the act of prayer. Now, he was no longer quite so sure.

An old saying from an ancient war held that there were no atheists in foxholes. That no matter how strongly a man professed his disbelief, when the hammer came down and the bullets started flying, he broke down and started praying like a Carmelite. Dev had not yet been reduced to praying on his knees, perhaps because he simply could not bring himself to believe that it would help, any more than the booze and pills did, but at least the booze and pills served to help deaden his emotions, like an anesthetic. He had, however, started talking to a priest. A Roman collar. A man named Father Liam Casey, Steele's close friend and confessor.

He had first gone to Father Casey because of the priest's relationship with Steele. He had, of course, not expected Father Casey to reveal anything that Steele had said in the confessional, just as he could not reveal anything that Steele said to him during their sessions together, but the two men were close friends, and, in a way, both Father Casey and Dev Cooper were working both sides of the same street. Dev was Steele's therapist, Father Casey his spiritual advisor.

Steele was not a deeply religious man. He was a "fallen Catholic," a man who had not attended church regularly since he had been a boy, a man who had made his own peace with himself and with his deity, lingering doubts and all, but some things died hard and never all the way.

Before Steele had become a cyborg, when he found himself feeling lost and confused, awash in self-doubt and guilt over his disintegrating marriage, he had wandered into St. Vincent's one day and made his way to the confessional, where Father Casey had sat behind the screen. He had started to confess, haltingly, but it hadn't quite worked out. At least, not in the traditional way. He had felt awkward in the darkened booth, uncomfortable with the ritual, ill at ease at not being able to see the face of the man he was unburdening his soul to. So Father

Casey, who was in many ways a rather different sort of priest, had suggested that they continue their "discussion" over a few beers in the bar across the street, and that had marked the beginning of their friendship.

Dev Cooper had gone to see him in the hope of furthering his understanding of his patient, who despite their fairly good relationship, had a deeply ingrained mistrust of psychiatrists and had never really opened up to Dev. Instead, Dev wound up opening up to Liam Casey.

"I'm not a Catholic," had been one of the first things that he told the priest.

The priest had smiled and said, "Hell, nobody's perfect."

Father Liam Casey was of medium height and stocky, with an athletic build, short blond hair and beard and incredibly alert, light green eyes that were flecked with gold. He was in his early 50s, though he looked younger, and with the exception of his collar, he made no concessions to priestly fashion, preferring to dress casually in tweed sport coats, jeans and western boots. Though he had no official clearance with the Steele Project, nor was he involved with it in any way beyond his personal relationship with Steele, the agency had checked him out most carefully, and Higgins had determined that Father Casey posed no security risk.

Nevertheless, Dev was well aware that he had told the priest far more than he should have. He had not told him all at once. Strictly speaking, the confidentiality of the confessional could not apply to Dev, since he was not a Catholic and thus could not go to confession, but as Dev got to know him better over the time they spent together, he became convinced that Father Casey could be trusted. Just the same, lately, his paranoia was increasing. He imagined agents following him everywhere with bolometric mikes and God only knew what other devilish devices, listening to his every word. He had taken to meeting Father Casey in very public places where there was a lot of covering noise. Usually a bar.

For his part, Liam Casey was concerned about Dev Cooper. They had known each other for only a short time, but both of them were the sort of men who were able to judge character, and they had soon developed a strong mutual trust and liking for each other. Father Casey saw Dev Cooper unravelling before his very eyes. Cooper's nerves were shot. It was not immediately visible, because Dev Cooper kept himself well in hand, but Liam Casey noticed how much he had been drinking, noticed the telltale signs of growing pill dependency, noticed the frantic desperation lurking deep in Cooper's eyes. And the worst part of it was that he had no answers for him.

When Steele had first come to him after his transformation, Steele had been concerned about his own humanity and seeking reassurance. Father Casey had told him that there were no easy answers, but he had been able to help Steele find answers of his own. Answers that, for Steele, for the time being at any rate, seemed to suffice, despite the lingering doubts. With Dev, it was much harder. Dev Cooper had presented him with a problem that seemed insurmountable, and Liam Casey understood why it had driven him to such a state.

Increasingly, they discussed theology. Dev Cooper, the scientist and secular philosopher, could not believe in God, yet it seemed suddenly important to him that he try. He played devil's advocate, dismantling his own attempts at faith, struggling to have it proved to him somehow beyond all doubt and argument that God existed, that there was "something higher," a rational order to the universe. He could not make the leap of faith. He seemed determined to hang onto the ladder of his pragmatism, but Dev, a deeply ethical and moral man, needed to believe in *something*, and his secular worldview no longer seemed enough.

It was not Liam Casey's mission to convert him, though many of his fellow priests might have disagreed with that. Liam Casey did not become a priest in order to become a missionary, in order to "sell" God. He became a priest because he found his greatest satisfaction in trying to do good. Helping people was his calling, the way he served his God. Most often, he helped them in his role as Catholic priest, but there were times when he merely helped them as a man, without imposing judgments or conditions.

He was well read and educated, with a lay knowledge of

psychiatry, philosophy and ethics, and he could discourse with erudition on a wide variety of subjects—none of which could serve him to help Dev. Dev's problem was unique. And it had become Liam Casey's problem, too, a problem that he could not share with anybody else, because, though Dev was not a Catholic, Dev had come to him in trust, and he owed it to him to give him the same confidentiality that he would give to his parishioners who came to him for confession. Together, they struggled to resolve a problem for which no solution seemed available.

Could a living, self-aware computer program have a human soul?

The young woman dancing on the stage not far from their table in the darkened corner was wearing nothing save a G-string and extremely thin high heels. From time to time, one of the customers seated at chairs placed around the perimeter of the stage would place a dollar bill on the apron, and she would saunter over to him, crouch down very close, so that his eyes were on a level with her barely covered genitalia. She would then pick up the money, roll it up to make a tube, and place it between the patron's teeth. Then, holding the G-string away from her, she would allow the patron to bend forward and, like a parrot with a seed, deposit the tip inside. Then she'd give him a quick kiss, bend backward, and proceed to thrust her crotch into his face, gyrating her pelvis as the man stared spellbound at the gate of hell.

It was an odd place to meet a priest, but Dev never picked the same place twice and this one had the virtue, albeit dubious, of having a sound system that was extremely loud and almost constant in its deafening assault. They could speak, but anyone attempting to eavesdrop on their conversation would never be able to make out what they said over the music.

The girl finished her obligatory three numbers, and as another girl climbed up on the stage to take her place, she came down and walked straight over to their table, her attention apparently caught by the only two men in the bar who were not paying attention to her.

"Hey, how come you two are being so shy back here? Would you like a table dance?"

And then she noticed Liam's collar and her eyes went wide.

"No thank you, dear," said Liam, slipping her a tip. "I'm just helping my friend here with a little family counseling, if you know what I mean. But you can be a love and bring us two more drinks."

"Oh, yeah, sure," she said. She glanced at Dev. "Listen, honey, if you're having a little trouble getting it turned on, stop by and see me later. I get off at ten. I do a little family counseling, too."

She turned and swiveled off toward the bar on her high heels.

"Friendly girl," said Liam.

"Look, maybe this wasn't such a good idea," Dev said. "We can find another place."

"No, no, that's all right, this place is fine," said Liam. "They water down their drinks a bit, but if they do it one more time, I'll send them back and threaten to excommunicate the bartender. Although watering yours down might not be such a bad idea. You've been hitting the sauce pretty hard lately."

"I know," said Dev. "I could always hold it pretty well, but it's starting to catch up with me."

"It's caught up with you and passed you," Liam said. "You look worse every time I see you."

"Yeah," said Dev. "It's getting so as I can hardly stand looking in the mirror anymore. For more reasons than one."

"I'm not your priest, Dev, and I certainly don't want to start sounding like your mother, but I *am* your friend. And as your friend, I'm telling you that you're in trouble. You're too good a psychiatrist to take refuge in denial. You need to get yourself under control. You need help."

"I know, Liam. But there isn't anywhere where I can go for help."

"Nonsense. You could check into a hospital. Or I could refer you to a support group, to counseling—"

"You think I don't know about all that?" said Dev. "Those aren't options I could consider. I'm part of a top-secret government project, Liam. And I've already compromised security by involving you."

"I was already involved before I even met you," Casey said, "because of Steele. Believe me, your Mr. Higgins left no stone unturned when he checked into my past. I've been interrogated, my friends have been questioned, my neighbors, my bishop, people whom I knew in childhood and attended seminary with. . . . I'm certain that they broke into my apartment and searched it thoroughly, though I can't prove it, and I'd be surprised if they didn't have my phone tapped. I couldn't be any more involved. And so far, the CIA is apparently satisfied that I do not pose a security risk. I'm far from what they would consider a team player, but I obviously don't worry them. If anyone can get in trouble out of all of this, it isn't me, it's you. You could lose your job."

"I sometimes wish I would," said Dev. "I sometimes wish I'd never taken it. But they won't cut me loose. They need me and I know too much. If they got really worried, I suppose there's a chance that they might kill me, but I doubt if it will come to that. Higgins knows I'd never jeopardize the project. It means too much to me. I'm like a junkie, Liam. I'm hooked. And I'm afraid."

"How can I help you, Dev? What can I do?"

"I don't know," said Cooper. "I guess it helps a lot just to have someone to talk to, someone who's not connected with the project."

The dancer came back and brought their drinks. Dev paid for them.

"Don't drink any more, Dev. Please."

Dev shook his head. "That's not the problem, Liam. The problem is that I can't drink enough. I don't know what to do about that program. Now Higgins has a copy, too. He knew I had it all along. He knew Gates gave it to me. He has my apartment bugged. I've looked everywhere, but I can't find them. He had someone come to my apartment and use my modem to send a backup download to him at project headquarters, so he could see what I've been doing with the program. He thinks that I've been fiddling with it, changing it. I told him that I hadn't, but I don't think he believed me. I tried to explain it to him and he acted as if he understood, but I don't really think he does. It's inconceivable that anyone could understand and not be terrified by the implications of it."

"What *are* the implications?" Liam asked.

"It goes beyond the moral question of whether or not we have a right to play at being Dr. Frankenstein," said Dev. "Nobody ever really thought this through. I have. I've been able to think of nothing else. They're all fascinated by the technology, like kids with a new toy. We can stick a little biochip into someone's brain and allow them to interface with a computer. Then we found out that we could use the biochip to download the information in a person's brain and store it in a computer as a mental engram matrix that could then be programmed into a cybernetic brain. But now we know that we can use that same technology to download mental engrams and duplicate them, back them up the same way you'd do with software, make an unlimited amount of copies. It terrifies me to think of what they might do with that technology.

"It would be like xeroxing human beings," continued Dev, growing more animated, "only they'd be electronic clones, self-aware and sentient personalities without bodies. In a sense, they'd almost be people just like us, only they'd be alive in some computer, existing only when they were booted up and then placed back into some sort of limbo, a suspended animation, a sort of electronic coma while they were in storage. They wouldn't be capable of feeling anything, or perhaps they would, who knows? Certainly not in the physical sense, but they would still have their *emotions*. The thoughts, the personalities of the original human being that they were duplicated from. How would *you* feel if you suddenly woke up one day to discover that you had no body, that you couldn't see or smell or touch, that you couldn't hear unless you were hooked up to an audio peripheral? That you couldn't speak unless a VS peripheral was attached? That you had been reduced to little more than an electronic slave, to be turned on and off at the will of the user? Liam, we'd be creating an entire sub-species of human beings, an electronic sub-species, people that had been reduced to software! It's more mind-boggling than any of the human experimental horrors carried on by the likes of Josef Mengele in World World II, more terrifying than the scare that swept across society when recombinant DNA technology first became possible! People were afraid that we'd wind up creating monsters. Yet that's exactly what we're doing now. It's what *I've* done. I've created a human, electronic, Frankenstein's monster! And the only way to uncreate it is to erase the program. And I could do that, but wouldn't it be murder, Liam? It would be like killing Steele."

"Does Steele know about the backup program?" Liam asked, a somber expression on his face.

"No, of course not," Dev said. "How could I possibly tell him? What do I say? There's another version of yourself backed up on my computer? And there's still another one in Higgins' office? We've already had one cyborg go insane, and Steele is having problems with the electronic ghosts within his matrix. Something like this could push him right over the edge."

"What are you going to do?" asked Liam.

"I don't know," said Dev, shaking his head. "I just don't know. *Would* it be murder to erase the program?"

Liam took a deep breath and let it out slowly. "I don't know, Dev. I just can't tell you. Under ordinary circumstances, no, of course it wouldn't be murder to erase a program, but these are human mental engrams. If you're asking me in my capacity as a priest, all I can tell you is that I don't think the Church would take the position that information downloaded from a human brain can be considered human, that it would have a soul. If you were a Catholic, and if the Church found out about this, they might well have you excommunicated. But if you're asking me as a man . . . well, then all I can tell you is that when I talk to Steele, I don't feel as if I'm talking to a machine. I feel as if I'm talking to the same man I knew before he was given a cybernetic brain transplant. But that's only how I feel. It's a question that theologians and philosophers, greater minds than ours, would probably argue about for years. Sometimes our feelings are all we have to go on."

"Even if it *would* be murder," Dev said, staring down into his glass, "perhaps it would be the kindest thing to do."

Liam shook his head. "I can't agree with that," he said. "I may not be your priest and you may not be Catholic, but I'm still concerned about your soul. I'll pray for you." He grimaced and then sighed. "You know, I never thought I'd hear myself say this, but for the first time in my life, those sound like empty words. Are you sure you're not the devil, Dev? You're starting to make me think like a secular humanist."

Dev smiled weakly. "Maybe I *am* the devil," he said. "Doesn't the Church say that God is within every one of us? Maybe the devil is, as well."

He waved for another drink. The girl started to come over, but Liam shook his head and waved her back. She shrugged and went back to attend to another customer.

"Don't, Dev," Liam said. "You've had enough."

"No," said Dev. "Not halfway near enough."

"I can't let you have another drink, Dev. I shouldn't have let you have the last one. It isn't going to help."

"I'll go get it myself then," Dev said, lurching to his feet.

Liam got up and took him by the arm. "Dev, please. It's not the answer."

"Answer?" Dev said. "I don't even know the question anymore. Come on, let go my arm, Liam."

"No, I'm not going to do that. You've have enough, Dev. Come on, let's go. Look, you can barely stand. Come back to my place and sleep it off. We'll talk more in the morning. Or let me take you home."

"No," said Dev. "It's waiting for me there. That program. That electronic clone. That Frankenstein's monster I created. Waiting with its questions and accusations. No, I'm not going home. I'm stayin' here. I'm gonna get good and drunk an' then talk to that nice girl about some of that counseling she offered."

Liam pulled on Dev's arm. "No, you're not. Come on, we're getting out of here."

"Let go of me," said Dev, shoving him away.

"Dev . . ."

"Go home, Liam. Leave me alone."

"I'm sorry, I can't do that."

"Well, fuck you then."

Dev turned away and started walking toward the bar. Liam caught up with him.

"Dev, please . . ."

"*Back off, God dammit!*" Dev shouted, shaking his hand off.

Liam sighed. "I'm sorry, Dev," he said, and smashed a right cross into Dev's jaw. He caught him as Dev started to crumple to the floor.

"Hey!" shouted the bartender.

"It's all right," said Liam. "My friend here's just had a bit too much to drink."

"Look, I don't want any goddamn trouble. . . . Oh, I'm sorry, Father. I didn't see the collar."

"It's all right, my son," said Liam. "I'll just take him home to sleep it off."

"Let me call you a cab, then I'll give you a hand with him when it gets here."

"Thank you. I appreciate that."

He lowered Dev into a booth and sat down beside him.

"Nice punch you got there, Father. Can I get you anything?" said the girl.

"No, thank you. I'll just wait for the cab."

"Sure you wouldn't like a table dance while you're waiting?"

"Get thee behind me," Liam said.

"Huh?"

He smiled. "Never mind. A small religious joke. Here, this is for your trouble."

"Thanks, hon. You come back and see me, 'kay?"

Father Casey smiled in spite of himself. Some people had no shame. He glanced at the unconscious man in the booth beside him and his smile faded. Dev Cooper, to his credit, wasn't one of them.

5

It was an ugly scene. By the time all the units got there, it was already over. The squad that spotted Stalker had picked him up near Grand and Orchard and had given pursuit, following him down to the Manhattan Bridge. Stalker fled from them, and they thought they had him on the run. But then he turned it all around on them. As Steele stood next to the melted and charred remains of one of the armored Strike Force pursuit vehicles, he could almost see how the action had played out.

Stalker had managed to stay just ahead of them, leading them down near the waterfront, beneath the elevated highway. Then he had turned and fought, taking out one vehicle with a plasma burst that charred and melted the SFP, superheating the pursuit car and cooking the unfortunate occupants as if they had been trapped inside an oven. Then the fuel cells had exploded and what was left of it was nothing more than a charred and smoking hulk, flames still licking from it, surrounded by partly melted pieces of shrapnel.

He had taken out the other SFP as well, and its remains were embedded in the front of an abandoned building, where it had crashed an instant before exploding. The armored van had also failed to escape destruction. The men inside had managed to get out just before the plasma hit, but they never had a chance to deploy. Some of them had been caught in the wash of plasma

flame and they lay on the ground, being given woefully
inadequate first aid by their fellow officers, who had arrived on
the scene too late to help them. Others had been cut down by
Stalker's laser. Some had died instantly, others lay upon the
cracked and buckled street, their bodies crushed. The para-
medic choppers came in and landed on the street, disgorging
men in white jumpsuits with stretchers. It looked like a war
zone.

"Christ, they never even had a chance," said Lt. Volkirk,
the commander of the federal squad that had just arrived on the
scene. He looked at the burning wreckage of the SFP's. "How
the hell do we stop a thing that can do that?"

Then he realized what he had said and gave Steele a quick,
embarrassed glance.

"Sorry, Lieutenant. I didn't mean that the way it sounded."

"Forget it," said Steele.

He was aware that a lot of the men were trying pointedly not
to look at him. This was what happened when a cyborg ran out
of control.

"He took their weapons," said Martinez, one of the other
officers. "Hell, it's not as if he was undergunned. *Look* at this,
for Christ's sake."

"Maybe he's running low on ammo," said Sgt. Kenealy.
"How many plasma charges does he have?"

"I don't know," said Steele. "We don't have any documen-
tation on his mods. He destroyed the data when he wiped out
the lab. But he can't have an indefinite supply."

"Maybe he didn't take them for himself," said Kenealy, a
veteran Strike Force cop.

They looked at him.

"What do you mean?" Volkirk asked.

Kenealy looked grim. "Out here, if he decided to recruit
himself an army, it's not as if there'd be any shortage of
volunteers."

"Christ, that's all we need," Volkirk said.

Steele frowned. "If you wanted to score yourself a lot of
weapons fast and you had the kind of ordnance that Stalker has,
where would you go?"

Kenealy gave him a sharp glance. "I'd hit the gangs," he said.

"This is Green Dragon turf," said Martinez. "Only how would he find them? They never keep their headquarters in the same location, and they're spread out all over the damn place."

"He'd do exactly what his name implies," said Steele. "He'd stalk them, like a guerrilla fighter. Mick often said that's just what we should do. Identify the gang members and take them out one at a time, or in groups of two and three, instead of trying to catch them in the act of breaking the law. Just hunt them down. Put the fear of God into 'em."

"I don't think God had anything to do with this," said Kenealy, looking around at the carnage, at his fellow officers being loaded into the choppers.

"He couldn't have gotten far," said Steele. "Concentrate all units in this area. I'm betting that he's going to hit the Dragons and either take their ordnance or force them to follow him. It's not the gangs he's after, it's me."

"Why you?" said Volkirk. "You guys were partners."

"Yeah," said Steele. "Maybe that's why. Mick Taylor's not Mick Taylor anymore. He's gone insane. He thinks I'm to blame for what's happened to him. Kenealy, I had to leave my place in one hell of a hurry, and after seeing what he's done here, I'm going to need more ordnance. I'll take your squad. You take my chopper and get back to my place. Tell Raven I'll need my full battle mods. She'll know what to give you. Then get back to me as soon as possible."

"Right. I'm on my way."

"Shit. As if things weren't bad enough," said Volkirk. He was looking up as a news chopper came in for a landing and Linda Tellerman came out, followed by her cameraman. She was dressed in a blue flightsuit with her station's logo stitched over her breast. "You want me to head her off?" asked Volkirk.

"Yeah, stall her till I'm out of here," said Steele. "I don't have time for this right now."

Another station's news chopper was hovering overhead, undoubtedly filming the scene of the battle, while two more news cars came screeching up.

"Lt. Steele!" shouted Linda Tellerman, as Volkirk came up to her.

Steele moved quickly to the chopper that had brought Kenealy's squad. "Mount up," he said to Kenealy's second in command, Sgt. Fossi. Fossi spoke into his helmet mike and the troops came running. Steele got into the chopper and moved up to sit next to the pilot. "Let's get the hell out of here," he said.

The battered gypsy cab pulled over to the curb at the corner of 110th and Fifth, near the northeast end of Central Park. The big black man got in the front seat, beside the driver. He was well over six feet tall, with the powerful frame of a body-builder. His twenty-four-inch arms strained the fabric of his custom-made black leather sport coat, and his chest was huge, with wide, flaring lats that tapered down to a slim, muscular waist. He shaved his head and he wore dark, black-rimmed sunglasses.

The driver of the cab was a grizzled old black man, skinny as a rake, with a deeply lined face and white stubble on his chin. He wore a shapeless, floppy leather cap and a wind-breaker over a dark red sweatshirt printed with dripping black letters that spelled out SEX AND VIOLENCE. His name was Slim, and in his younger days, he had been the leader of a Harlem street gang called the Skulls. The huge mountain of a man beside him had taken over as leader of the Skulls when Slim got too old to run a street gang and retired.

His physical appearance and his badly dented gypsy cab gave no clue to Slim's true financial status. Slim was more than comfortable. He was one of the most successful independent pimps in no-man's-land, with a small, exclusive stable of beautiful young girls who doted on him like a favorite uncle. Unlike most pimps, he treated his girls well and took good care of them. They didn't have to walk the streets. Slim had a well-heeled, white clientele which didn't mind paying extra for cab service to and from the apartment building where he kept his girls, right on the edge of no-man's-land.

"Watchya been doin', Ice?" said Slim in a husky, gravelly voice. "Feds treatin' ya right?"

It always amused Slim to no end that the scrappy youngster he had taken under his wing when he was leader of the Skulls had become a federal agent; given full amnesty, a job and a luxurious apartment in exchange for his assistance in helping Steele take down Victor Borodini.

"I got no complaints," said Ice. When he spoke, he sounded like the voice of doom. His voice was deep and resonant, and anybody hearing it without actually seeing him, such as over the phone, knew immediately that it came from something *big*. Ice reached into his jacket pocket and took out a small photograph. He handed it to Slim.

"Seen this girl around?"

"Workin' girl?" asked Slim, taking the photo of Cory Steele.

"That's what I hear," said Ice.

Slim examined the photo. "Young blood. Haven't seen her. Mind if I ask what your interest is?"

"Personal," said Ice. "The girl be Steele's daughter."

Slim gave a low whistle. "Whoo, boy. Someone done bought into one *pack* o' trouble. Her player know who she is?"

"I doubt it," Ice said. "Otherwise, he crazy."

"She strung out?"

"Don't know. Last time she be seen, it be right here on this corner."

Slim shook his head. "This ain't nobody's private strip," he said. "She workin' it?"

"Meetin' someone. Her brother. She wanted out, but her player showed up and beat the tar outta the kid. Messed him up good."

"So the kid saw him then."

"Yeah, but he ain't in no shape to talk about it. Soon's I get me a description, I get back to you."

"Steele out lookin' for her now?"

Ice shook his head. "Steele got much bigger problems."

"More important than his little girl?"

Ice turned to face Slim slowly. "Man ain't got no choice,"

he said. "Raven say he torn up about it pretty bad. I lookin' into this on his behalf. I owe the man."

"I'll see what I can do," said Slim. He held up the photo. "Can I keep this?"

"Do that."

"Kay. I get right on it. What's her name?"

"Cory."

"What happens if I find her? You want me to talk to her main man? Convince him he be makin' a big mistake he don't let her go?"

"He already made a big mistake," said Ice. "You find her, you stay out of it. Call me."

"You got it."

"Thanks, Slim," said Ice. He reached for his wallet.

"Hey, son, you not gonna insult me, are ya?"

Ice took his hand out of his jacket.

"That's better," Slim said. "Go on. Get outta here. I gots work to do."

There were many places in the city where the creatures from the underworld could come up from their tunnels. Most of them were deep in no-man's-land, the ghetto ruins surrounding Midtown. The mortality rate in no-man's-land was high. People often disappeared. Mothers cried at night over their lost children, knowing they'd never be seen again. The unfortunates who lived in no-man's-land were trapped by poverty and circumstance in a desolate existence that offered no hope for improvement and not much for survival. Many of them were dead already, though their bodies hadn't realized it yet. They shambled through the streets, fueled by drugs, booze and insanity, no longer caring if the hammer fell or not. And many of them were mean, taught by the dictates of survival in the urban jungle to scratch and claw for their existence like savage beasts. The Green Dragons were among the meanest of the lot.

Many, though by no means all, of them were Asian. The Dragons were the linear descendants of the gangs that once ruled Chinatown. They controlled the makeshift economy of their blasted section of the ghetto. They controlled the shabby little businesses, they controlled the prostitution, they controlled the crime. They got a cut of everything that happened on their turf, and if they didn't, it soon ceased to happen. Permanently.

At one time, they had come under the control of Victor Borodini, head of the most powerful crime enclave on Long Island. There had been no need for Victor Borodini to subdue them to his will. He was, as he often styled himself, a businessman, and he had simply offered them a deal that they could not refuse. From his dealings with the freebooters and with corrupt politicians, Borodini had almost unlimited access to two commodities that were very highly valued on the Dragon's turf. Guns and drugs. He promised to supply them with all they needed in return for a modest percentage of their action and an occasional job he wanted done.

The Dragons thought it was good business. And, for a while, it had been. But now that the Borodini enclave was in federal hands and Victor Borodini in hiding, the Dragons were once more on their own. They'd been approached by Borodini's men, but they were no longer interested. They had plenty of guns cached throughout their turf, and there was no shortage of illegal drugs.

The Delano family, from Brooklyn, had wasted little time in taking up the slack. Anthony Delano had no political axe to grind. He only wanted profit, so the deal was not quite as attractive as the one that Borodini offered them. There was no percentage action. It was just straight business. Buy and sell. But that was okay, too. It was still good business.

Three of the Dragons walked together down the cracked and buckled sidewalk, heading for their clubhouse. They moved the clubhouse often, just to keep the cops off balance. Unlike the Skulls, up north in Harlem, they didn't stick to the same places, daring the Strike Force cops to come in and try to get them. The Dragons were craftier. They stayed mobile. They never kept all their action in one place. And only the members knew where the next meeting would be held.

The three young toughs all carried Chinese AK-47s. In the days before the Bio-War, there had been a flood of such weapons coming into the States from Beijing, manufactured in factories scattered throughout China and exported to the European and American civilian markets. They were well made and relatively inexpensive, compared to similar European and domestic ordnance, the result of cheap skilled labor with minimal automation, and the Kalashnikov design was strong and reliable. They were also fairly easily convertible to illegal, fully automatic fire. Through Victor Borodini, the Dragons had gotten hold of a large shipment of them, stored for years in warehouses in the south and picked up by some freebooter. They also had Chinese copies of the U.S. M-14 and the Russian Tokarev pistol. Nor was that the only ordnance available to the street gangs in no-man's-land.

In the years before the Bio-War, there had been a concerted effort to ban firearms, especially handguns. Fully automatic weapons were the first to go, largely because it was difficult, if not impossible, for a case to be made for their use as sporting arms. Consequently, first came stringent licensing requirements, then an outright ban. Then came the ban on so-called "assault rifles," semi-automatic weapons based on military designs, since they were capable of being fitted with large capacity magazines and could be illegally altered to fully automatic function. Small handguns were the next to be legislated against. Christened "Saturday Night Specials," a name originally coined to apply to cheaply made, inexpensive, small caliber handguns, the term was gradually expanded to apply to any short barreled handgun that was easily concealable, regardless of design or price or quality of manufacture. The argument was made that the only conceivable purpose for such weapons was to kill people, since they were of no practical use in hunting and not accurate enough for target shooting. Consequently, it was stated that no one except police and military personnel had any business owning them. Larger handguns were the next logical step, and banning them was easier once the other weapons were prohibited. After all, a .44 Magnum or a .357 with a 6″ barrel could still be concealed beneath a coat or jacket. The result of all this supposedly well-intentioned legislation was a booming black market in illegal weapons, either imported or illegally manufactured domestically.

It was similar to what happened during the days of Prohibition, when anyone who possessed a bathtub could make gin. The manufacture of a firearm was not a very complicated process. Anyone with a well set up machine shop could turn out illegal weapons, and there was a proliferation of them, in varying degrees of quality. And the drug runners found another lucrative commodity to deal in. For that matter, any kid could make a "zip gun" from a broken car antenna, some electrician's tape, a rubber band and a block of wood. All the legislation managed to accomplish was to take guns out of the hands of law-abiding citizens. It affected criminals not at all and did not significantly alter crime statistics. What it did was create a new and highly profitable illegal industry.

The crime families went into the arms business in a big way. And, just as with drugs, many of their illegally manufactured products were soon well known by evocative street names— Jaguar, Kodiak, Demon, Viper and many others. After the Bio-War, when a beleaguered populace forced the repeal of the gun laws, many of the "gunleggers" became legitimate, among them companies such as American Small Arms and Mongoose Industries. Throughout history, wherever there was a demand, there always arose inevitable outlets of supply, and the street gangs had a wide array of firearms to choose from.

In addition to their AK-47s, the three young men also carried 9mm. Viper machine pistols in large holsters on their belts, along with several spare magazines holding 20 rounds apiece. Over their street gang colors, they wore weapons harnesses, incorporating shoulder holsters for semiautomatic pistols—one of them carried a .45 caliber Demon, the other two each had a 9mm. Mongoose—along with magazine pouches and nylon sheaths for their commando knives.

The three gang members looked like a cross between mercenaries and Caribbean pirates. Aside from their colors, black denim vests brilliantly embroidered with the design of a green Chinese dragon on the back, they wore loose black martial arts trousers or camo fatigues tucked into paratrooper boots, bright sweatshirts or no shirts at all, long hair held in place by colorful silk scarves rolled up into headbands, earrings, studded bracelets, rings, chains, amulets and intricate Chinese tattoos.

It was starting to grow dark as they sauntered arrogantly down the street, but they were confident that they were well enough equipped to deal with any threat they might encounter. They were wrong.

Stalker dropped down from a second story window, landing right behind them. As they spun around, he grabbed the rifle from the nearest one and smashed its butt into the Dragon's face, bursting flesh and pulverizing bone. He kicked out with his foot and broke the second Dragon's kneecap. The young man cried out and collapsed to the sidewalk. The third one brought up his AK-47, but he never had the chance to fire. Stalker fired the rifle he'd grabbed from his first victim, and the Dragon flew backward as the spray of bullets caught him in the chest. Then Stalker turned back to the Dragon with the broken knee.

The young man had dropped his rifle and it now lay out of reach. Grimacing with pain, he pulled out his machine pistol and fired point blank, emptying the magazine. Stalker jerked and staggered backward as the bullets struck him in the chest, but they didn't put him down. The Dragon held his empty weapon and stared with disbelief as the man kept coming at him. He fumbled for a spare magazine, but as he tried to insert it into the machine pistol, Stalker bent down and easily plucked the weapon from his grasp, tossing it behind him. As the Dragon tried to reach for the pistol in his shoulder holster, Stalker grabbed his hand and squeezed. There was a crunching, crackling sound, and the Dragon screamed with pain as his hand was crushed.

Stalker released his mangled hand and grabbed the weapons harness. He gave a sharp yank and the Dragon cried out as the harness broke. Stalker turned around and tossed it to one of the shabby men behind him, along with the captured rifle. The Dragon noticed them for the first time. It was as if they had come out of nowhere. They were bending down over the bodies of his friends and relieving them of their weapons. Then, to his horror, they started to drag the bodies away, a hungry look in their bright, demented eyes.

Stalker bent down over him. "Where's the meeting?" he said.

The Dragon didn't answer.

Stalker reached out with one finger and popped the Dragon's left eye out of its socket, then tore it loose. The Dragon's agonized scream echoed through the streets.

Stalker held the eye up. "I said, where's the meeting?"

Blood leaking down his face, the Dragon shook his head. "No . . . please! No more! I'll tell you!"

"*Where?*"

The Dragon told him.

Stalker straightened up and turned to the disheveled men gathered behind him.

"He's all yours."

"*No! No, don't! Please! No!*"

The throat-rending scream echoed through the streets as the derelicts descended on their victim like a pack of hungry wolves, and then it was cut off abruptly.

"Come on, let's go," said Rico. "I've got a special customer for you tonight. He likes 'em young and tender."

"No," said Cory, staring fully at the floor. "I'm not going."

"What was that?"

"You heard me," she said tonelessly. "I'm not going. I can't do it anymore. I won't. It's disgusting!"

Rico's eyes glittered as he stared down at her. He stood over her, dressed in a long black cabretta leather coat, black suede boots with high spike heels, skin tight black lycra pants and a flowing, ruffled white shirt, open at the neck to reveal a dozen gold chains and amulets. His black hair was streaked with silver and it hung down to his shoulders. At first glance, he could easily have been mistaken for a woman. He was very pretty, with olive skin and dark almond eyes. He wore a dangling, silver crucifix in his left ear, and his hands were studded with gold and diamond rings. He lashed out suddenly, giving her a stinging slap across the face and tangling his fingers in her long blond hair.

She cried out as he pulled her off the bed and dragged her to the floor by her hair, getting down on one knee beside her, bringing his perfumed face close to hers.

"You'll do what I tell you, bitch!" he snarled. "Or do you want more of what you got the last time?"

Cory gasped with pain and blinked back tears. "I don't care!" she said defiantly. "I don't care what you do to me! I'm not gonna do it anymore! It's ugly! It's disgusting!"

"*You're* ugly!" Rico hissed, putting his face up close to hers and yanking sharply on her hair. "*You're* disgusting! You're nothing but a common little tramp! A slut! You'll do what I tell you, you little whore, or I'll rip your goddamn lungs out!"

He let go of her hair and slapped her once again. Cory huddled on the floor, sobbing.

"You'll be sorry!" she said. "You just wait! You'll be sorry when my daddy finds you!"

"Your daddy," Rico said with derision. "Your daddy's probably been putting it to you since you were nine."

"He has not!" cried Cory, tears streaming down her face. "He's going to get you for what you've done to me! You'll be sorry! He's a cop! A Strike Force cop!"

Rico snorted. "Is he, now?"

"His name's Lt. Steele and he's the best cop on the force! He'll find you and he'll make you pay!"

"Steele?" Rico said, his eyes growing wide. "Not Lt. Donovan Steele?"

"That's right!" said Cory. "And if you don't let me go, he'll find you and he'll *kill* you!"

"Shut up!" Rico said, backhanding her viciously across the face. Cory cried out again and huddled in a little ball on the floor, her arms up over her head as she sobbed.

Rico stared down at her for a long moment, then turned to one of the other girls. "You'll do her trick tonight," he said.

"Sure, baby. Anything you say."

Rico went over to the phone. He picked it up and dialed. "This is Rico," he said. "Let me talk to Ricky B. Tell him it's important. *Real* important." He waited a moment. "Mr. Borodini? How you doin'? Yeah, I said it was important. You'll be glad I called. I've got a big surprise for you. A real big surprise."

He glanced over at Cory, huddled on the floor, and smiled.

The lab on level B–3 of the Federal Building was a bustle of activity. The wreckage caused by Stalker when he had broken out had been removed, and new equipment was being brought in. With crews working around the clock, most of the physical damage had already been repaired, and teams of technicians were busily at work installing new programs and trying to retrieve the damaged data. Higgins watched Dr. Jennifer Stone, who had been brought out from Los Alamos to replace the late Dr. Phillip Gates.

She was young, in her mid-thirties, a redhead with bright green eyes who was uncomfortably pretty, though she took no pains to emphasize her beauty. But then, she didn't need to, Higgins thought. She looked much better than her photograph, which had caused Higgins to raise his eyebrows when he looked over her file. Dev Cooper had worked with her at Los Alamos and he had a very high opinion of her. Almost too high.

"Was there ever anything personal between you?" Higgins had asked, watching Cooper carefully.

Dev had smiled and shook his head. "No," he said, "but it wasn't for lack of tryin'. She's a real knockout, isn't she? But I don't think I was her type."

"What is her type?" said Higgins.

"I don't really know," said Dev. "Maybe she doesn't have one. Hell, just about every guy on the project took his best shot at one time or another, even the married ones, but so far's I know, she never gave any of 'em a tumble. Some thought she might be gay, but there was no real indication of it. She's real discreet. Keeps her personal life personal."

Higgins had nodded. "That speaks well of her. What about her attitude? She a team player, or is she the independent sort, like you?"

Dev had chuckled. "She's very, very serious," he said. "Aggressive, ambitious, and thoroughly professional. If you're asking if she'll rock the boat, I'd say that should be the least of your worries. Politically, she's almost as much of a fascist as you are. In other words, I don't think you'll have to worry about her being lax about security. She ran her section of the lab like a Gestapo colonel."

"Really?" Higgins said. "Her file is impressive. The most impressive of all the candidates we've screened. So you think she'd fit in well?"

"Oh, she'll fit in, all right," said Dev. "But if you don't watch your ass, she'll have your job within a year."

Higgins had called her personally to offer her the job. When he had asked her how soon she could get there, she said she'd be on the next flight. She was. She had arrived with just one suitcase, but so far as Higgins knew, she hadn't even seen the apartment he'd arranged for her yet. She had moved into her office, which had once belonged to Gates, and she used the bathroom and shower facilities in the gym. She had plunged right in immediately, taking charge like a commando. And anyone who didn't give one hundred percent heard the whip cracked and snapped to. Higgins was impressed. She saw him watching her and came over.

"Something?" she said.

"Just came down to see how you were doing."

"We're making good progress," she said. "It's still too early to tell if we'll be able to retrieve all the damaged data, but we're working on it. Any word from the people in the field?"

The field. She meant the streets. She even talked like a commando, Higgins thought.

"Yeah, and it's not good," he said. "Stalker was spotted by one of the Strike Force units. They engaged pursuit and he took them out so fast they didn't know what hit them. And now we've lost him once again."

She nodded curtly. "Gates did good work," she said. "Too bad he was so sloppy about keeping backup records."

"Gates was a brilliant man, but he was sloppy about a lot of things," said Higgins. "When you get a chance, there's something I'd like for you to check out for me."

"Is it important? I've got a lot to do here."

"It could be. I'm not sure," said Higgins. "You seen Dr. Cooper yet?"

"Yes, he stopped by briefly." She paused. "He looks like hell."

"He's been under a lot of strain," said Higgins.

"Is that what happens to people on this project?" she said. "They either get killed or fall apart?"

"I'm still here and in one piece," said Higgins with a smile.

"Because you have other people do the dirty work?"

"Maybe. You say what's on your mind, don't you?"

"Not always. Only when it helps save time. What's bugging Dev? He's one of the most stable, centered people I've ever known, but it's obvious that he's been drinking heavily, and I think he's also taking drugs. He shows all the signs. I've seen that sort of thing before."

"It has to do with Steele," Higgins said. "And with that problem I just mentioned to you."

"If it's doing that to him, then it must be one hell of a problem," she said.

"I don't want to take any time away from what you're doing here," said Higgins, "but I'd appreciate your input on this."

She pursed her lips thoughtfully. "You going to be around tonight? Late, I mean."

"I can be."

"Good. I'll be sending some of my people home around ten. I've got them working shifts, but we've got a hole in the schedule between ten and four, to allow the work crews time to finish up and install the rest of the equipment. I'll meet you in your office at ten-thirty, if that will be convenient."

"That'll be fine. You working straight through?"

"There's a lot to do."

"We don't want to wear you out," said Higgins.

"Don't worry. You won't."

It was almost one o'clock in the morning when Jennifer got up from the computer in Higgins' office. She didn't look in the least bit tired, despite the fact that she'd been on her feet since four A.M. Her green eyes were bright with excitement.

"This is fantastic," she said. "Dev was right. It *is* self-aware!"

"You're absolutely sure?" said Higgins, frowning.

"Beyond a doubt," she said. "Dev Cooper couldn't have done this. Not even with the help of someone like Gates. The program is alive. It's responding in a completely human manner. It *thinks*. It's got a personality!"

"Steele's personality," said Higgins. "Cooper talks to it."

"He *talks* to it?"

"Through a VS peripheral," Higgins said. "Gates programmed it for him. Made it sound like Steele."

"Of course," she said. "It makes perfect sense. Dev's a psychiatrist. He'd be able to relate to it much easier that way. Christ, no wonder he's such a wreck. Do you have any idea what this *means*?"

"I'm not sure I do, exactly," Higgins said.

"It means you have the capability to duplicate human intelligence," she said excitedly. "It's an absolutely shattering scientific breakthrough! Gates must have been blind not to have realized what you had here. Either that, or he simply didn't want to see it."

"Why wouldn't he want to see it?" Higgins asked, puzzled.

"Maybe it was subconscious," she said. "A function of self-preservation. Dev Cooper saw it and look what it's done to him. It's made him a nervous wreck."

"Yeah, Cooper said something like that. But it doesn't seem to have disturbed you all that much," said Higgins.

"Are you kidding? Look at me! I'm practically shaking! This is the most exciting thing that's ever happened to me! I'm on an incredible adrenaline high! You've *got* to let me work on this!"

"I still don't fully understand," said Higgins. "Slow down a little and explain it to me. Have a drink?"

"Vodka," she said. "Straight and neat."

"Coming right up." He went over to the bar in his office.

She was pacing back and forth, running her fingers through her hair. She was incredibly wired.

"The implications of this are mind-boggling!" she said.

"There's practically no limit to what you could do with something like this!"

"Give me a for instance," he said, handing her the drink. He took his usual Scotch, sat down and lit a cigarette. He offered her one and she took it, inhaling on it manically.

"How would you like to be in several dozen places at the same time," she said, "running several dozen different operations simultaneously? In effect, with this, you could! You could clone yourself, electronically, and operate out of computers in different parts of the country, all networked together, reporting to you right here in your office! What we've been doing in Los Alamos, what you started doing here, is only the tip of the iceberg. I can't believe it never occurred to any of us to try this!" She shook her head. "But it was so far fetched. . . . it was staring us in the face all along and we just didn't see it! God, how stupid! We've only been experimenting with downloading limited bits of information, being typically conservative, taking tiny little steps, when Gates, God bless him, took a giant leap and outdistanced us all! We've all been suffering from tunnel vision. We've been too cautious. Jesus!"

She emptied her glass and came around to the front of the desk, resting her hands on it and bending forward toward him, her eyes dancing with excitement.

"What Gates did was to download all the information from Steele's brain and store it until it could be programmed back into the cybernetic brain that you gave Steele. And, being the engineer he was, he kept a backup. But he never did anything with it! That's what's so amazing. That he never explored the possibilities! He kept just one. He never thought of it as anything more than just another piece of software. He was wedded to the idea that it was the hardware, the cybernetic brain, that made it work, but a computer can make it work equally well, because it doesn't matter. *The software is the thing!* A human mental engram matrix, alive and self-aware! And you can make copies of it. *Limitless* copies! You can take one Steele and create an *army* of them, all with the same personality, all capable of interaction, all thinking and responding the same way! And you could do it with anyone! Soldiers, scientists, political leaders, corporate executives . . . do you see where it could lead?"

Higgins gave a low whistle. "That never even occurred to me," he said.

"It never occurred to anyone else who knew about this, either," she said, "except Dev Cooper. You all became so caught up in the Steele project that you never realized that the original aim of Project Download has been realized! This is it! You've succeeded, Higgins! You've pulled it off! You've created the ultimate synthesis of human and computer intelligence! And I'm right here on the ground floor! It's the opportunity of a lifetime! I could kiss you for giving me this job!"

Higgins stared at her. Her thick red hair was in disarray, her eyes were bright, she was practically glowing with energy and excitement.

"I wouldn't stop you," he said.

She stared at him. Then she suddenly reached across the desk, grabbed him by his necktie and roughly pulled him close to her. Their lips met and her mouth opened, her tongue eagerly seeking his. She sat down on the desk and lay back, pulling him down with her, her fingers clutching roughly at his hair. Things fell off the desk as he bent down over her, running his hands over her lush body, down to her legs and up her dress. They wasted no time with preliminaries. They were both out of control. He had her right there on the desk, with her dress up around her waist and her long legs wrapped around him.

And all the while, the screen on the computer glowed. They didn't notice when several of the other screens across the room, in the large wall console, came on suddenly and started flashing data at an astonishing rate. They didn't notice when the surveillance camera mounted near the ceiling in the corner of the room silently pivoted around and focused on them. Another screen in the wall console came on, showing them locked together, kissing passionately and thrusting against each other. And then, one by one, the screens winked out. But the camera remained focused upon them.

6

When Jason Steele woke up, the biggest, meanest looking black man he'd ever seen was standing at the foot of his bed, looking down at him.

"How you feelin', kid?" said Ice.

"Better," Jason said, a bit nervously, through swollen lips. "Who're you?"

"Friend o' your daddy's. Name's Ice."

"Are you a cop?"

Ice smiled. "Not hardly." He sat down on the edge of the bed. "Feel up to talkin' much?"

"Yeah, I guess so. Where's my father?"

"He be back soon as he can. Meanwhile, we gotta see what we can do 'bout findin' your little sister. You remember the man that worked you over?"

"Yeah," said Jason, bitterly. "I remember him *real* well."

"What he look like?"

"Tall and slim, about six-foot-four or so, but he was wearing real high heels," Jason said. "Boots, but the kind a girl would wear, you know? Dark skin, but not black. Hispanic, I think. Or maybe Italian. Young guy, in his twenties. Real long black hair, with silver streaks in it, a long black leather trench coat, tight pants, ruffled shirt, lot of chains and rings. . . . I remember the rings especially," he said, touching his battered face. "Weird eyes. Scary looking."

Ice grimaced. "Want you should take a look at somethin'," he said. He picked up one of the mug books that the police sent over and flipped through the pages. "This him?"

He showed Jason the photograph.

"Yeah! That's him! That's the guy!"

Raven stuck her head through the door. "He awake?"

"Yeah," said Ice, shutting the book and putting it down.

"You feel like eating something, Jason?" she said. "How about some soup? You need to get your strength up."

"Some soup would be nice. Thank you, Miss Scarpetti."

"Just call me Raven, hon. We don't have be so formal. I'll go put some on for you."

"I be back later," Ice said. "Take it slow."

He followed Raven out into the kitchen.

"How's he doing?" she asked.

"He be okay," said Ice.

"He tell you anything about the creep that did it?"

"Yeah," said Ice. "I know who it is."

She glanced at him sharply. "Who?"

"Your old friend, Rico."

Her eyes went wide. "Jesus. Are you sure?"

"Kid I.D.'d his mug shot. I think I go pay the man a call," said Ice.

"I'm going with you."

"Not a good idea," Ice said. "'Sides, someone gotta stay here with the boy."

"I'd like to tear his eyes out with my bare hands," Raven said savagely. "The things that bastard put me through, the things he made me do. . . ." She took a deep breath. "When I think of Steele's daughter being with him. . . ." She clenched her fists.

"Maintain, girl," Ice said. "I bring her back, don't worry."

"*Hurt* him for me, Ice," Raven said through gritted teeth. "Kill the son of a bitch."

"Count on it," said Ice.

He turned and went out the door.

That poor kid, Raven thought. She knew just how it must have happened. She got picked up by one of Rico's "talent scouts," a kindly looking, well-dressed older man with a soft voice and good manners, anxious over a young girl who seemed to be in trouble. . . . She could imagine how Cory Steele must have felt when she realized, too late, the terrible mistake that she had made. Rico would have raped her, brutally. He always did, to break down their defenses. Just as he had done with her. After that first time, he never touched his girls again, except to punish them or keep them in line, but that first time was something that would stay with Cory for the rest of her life. She'd never be the same again. Rico was a real twist.

Her hands trembled as she made the soup for Jason. She remembered her own introduction to "the life." She had been Tommy Borodini's girl, living at the enclave out in Cold Spring Harbor, very young, not quite sixteen. Tommy had seemed glamorous. He was good looking, fun to be with, rich. He'd taken her out in high style and she thought she was in love. Until the day she caught Tommy in bed with one of her best friends. They'd fought and Tommy had struck her repeatedly. She had laid his face open with a knife and that had sealed her fate. He'd beaten her bloody, then turned her over to his thugs. Those animals had gone at her for hours, until she thought she'd lose her mind, and all the time, Tommy had sat there, watching. Yet that was not the end of it. The worst was still to come.

They threw her in a car and drove her to the city, out to no-man's-land. And they had given her to Rico as a present, on Tommy Borodini's orders. By the time Rico was through "indoctrinating" her, she had no resistence left. But in time, she started to defy him, and even Rico finally decided she was more trouble than she was worth. She thought he'd kick her out, but she had underestimated his cruelty. He had turned her over to the Skulls. They took her to that warehouse where Victor Borodini stored his weapons and his drugs. Steele came with Ice to bust the place and found her being gang-raped by the Skulls. He'd rescued her and she'd been with him ever since, at first only to help him get Tommy Borodini, and later, after Tommy B. was dead, because she didn't ever want to be with anybody else.

She didn't think of him as being a cyborg, part man and part machine. It didn't matter to her that he had a cybernetic brain. The only thing that mattered to her was that Steele was the first man she'd ever met who treated her as if she were a *person*, a human being with some worth. He didn't care about what she had been, what she had done or what had been done to her. And it hadn't taken very long at all for her to fall in love with him.

Earlier that day, an officer had come back to pick up Steele's battle mods. Now he was out there somewhere, hunting another cyborg like himself, a man who had once been his partner and best friend, while his son lay bruised and battered and his daughter was in the hands of a psychopathic pimp whose savage cruelty Raven knew all too well. What must he be feeling? How would he be able to do what he had to do with all that on his mind? She was afraid for him. And she was afraid for Cory.

She poured the soup into a bowl, and trying to compose herself, she took it in to Jason. She found him out of bed and halfway dressed.

"What do you think you're doing?" she said, putting the soup down on the nightstand.

"I'm going out to look for Cory," he said.

"Like hell you are," she said. "Get back in bed."

"Don't try to stop me," he said. "I appreciate what you're doing, but—"

"But nothing," she said, taking him by the shoulders and pushing him gently but firmly back down on the bed. "You're not going anywhere. You're gonna stay right here and rest. The doctor said you shouldn't move much till you get some X-rays, and I'm gonna make damn sure you stay put. I promised your father I'd look after you. Ice went to look for Cory. Don't worry. He'll find her and bring her back."

"He said my father had to go out on a job. . . ."

"That's right. Something real important came up."

"More important than finding his own daughter?" Jason said.

"Don't be that way. Your father had no choice. It tore his heart out to leave while Cory was still out there somewhere and in trouble, but there's a maniac out there who's killing people, and your father is the only one who can stop him."

"Why?"

"Because the killer is another cyborg. Only something went wrong with his brain and he's out of control. Your father's got to find him before he kills any more people. Ice knows where Cory is. He's gone to get her. He'll bring her back. And he'll make that bastard pay for what he's done."

Jason was silent for a moment.

"Who is he?" he said finally. "Is Ice his real name?"

"I don't know his real name," said Raven. She sat down on the bed beside him. "I don't think anybody does. He used to be the leader of a street gang called the Skulls."

"The *Skulls*?" said Jason, surprised. "But they're criminals!"

"He isn't with them anymore," said Raven. "He's working with your father now, for the government."

Jason shook his head. "So much has changed," he said. "I'm still confused." He moistened his lips. "My mother told us Dad was dead."

"I know," said Raven. "For what it's worth, Jason, I think she meant well. She just didn't understand."

"I'm not sure I do," Jason said. "I heard about him on the news. That's how Cory and I found out he was still alive. But I really don't know what to think. I mean, he looks and acts the same but . . . they say his brain is a computer now."

"That's right," said Raven. "But that doesn't make him a machine. At least, not as far as I'm concerned. He's still your father, Jason."

"What happened to him?"

"He was shot up real bad by Victor Borodini's men. When they brought him to the hospital, he was in coma. There was nothing they could do for him. But the man he works for, a CIA man named Higgins, had him brought to a lab in the

Federal Building. Your father was doing some work for the government. A secret project. They put a special chip into his brain as part of an experiment to see if people could link up with computers. After he was shot, they used that chip to take all the information from his brain, what they call mental engrams, and put it into a cybernetic brain that they replaced his real one with. I know it sounds pretty wild, but he's not a machine, Jason. He's just got some artificial parts, that's all, prosthetics, like somebody who's been in an accident or who's handicapped. But your mother didn't see it that way. Because one of those parts is a computer brain, she thought they'd turned him into some kind of robot. It scared her. I guess she just did what she thought was best. Here, eat some of this before it gets cold."

Jason started to eat, gingerly.

"You love him, don't you?" he said.

Raven nodded. "Yes, I love him very much," she said.

"How'd you meet him?"

She hesitated. "It's a long story," she said. "You know, you should call your mother, let her know you're here. She's worried about you."

"You spoke to my mother?"

"She came here looking for you and Cory, but your father told her to go back home and wait, just in case the two of you came back."

"I'm not going back," he said bitterly. "She lied to us. She told us Dad was dead. If she'd told us the truth, none of this would've happened!"

"People make mistakes, Jason," she said. "I know I've made my share. I'm not saying your mother was right doing what she did, but she still loves you. And she's worried sick about you."

"I don't want to talk to her," said Jason. "What happened to Cory is all her fault. I'll never forgive her for that."

"I can understand your anger," Raven said. "But you can't blame what happened to Cory on your mother. It's *not* her fault. It's the fault of that bastard, Rico."

He glanced up at her sharply. "Rico? You know his name?"

Raven sighed. "Yeah, I know his name," she said. She hesitated. "He used to be my pimp."

Jason stared at her. "Your *pimp*? You mean you're a. . . ." He stopped, flustered and embarrassed.

"A hooker," she said. "At least, that's what I was, before I met your father. It's part of that long story I told you about. I didn't choose to be a prostitute. I got trapped into it, a lot like Cory did. So I know exactly what she's going through right now. And it's pretty rough, believe me. We'll get her back, but she's gonna need a lot of help and understanding. She's gonna need you to be there for her. She's gonna feel dirty and ashamed. She might need to see a doctor for a while, to help her get through this. And she'll need her family behind her, givin' her love and support. She'll need you and your mother to be there for her, to be strong and be together."

"After what Mom did, I doubt she'll want to go back," said Jason.

"She'll want to go back," said Raven. "She'll need to go back. And we'll have to make your mother understand about what Cory's been through. It won't be easy. Believe me, knowing that will be punishment enough for her. Nobody should have to go through something like this. Nobody. Don't hate your mother. This whole thing is gonna bring her more pain than anyone deserves. Try to forgive her, Jason. Because for her sake and for Cory's, you're gonna have to help her to forgive herself."

Jason looked at her and smiled. "I can see why my dad likes you," he said. "You're a pretty special lady."

She smiled and kissed him on the cheek. "You're pretty special yourself, hon. If I had a brother, I'd want him to be just like you. Now why don't you call your mom and let her know you're safe?"

"Okay," he said. "But I'm going to wait until Ice comes back with Cory. You sure he can find her and bring her back? That Rico's pretty mean."

"Not half as mean as Ice," said Raven. "He'll bring her back, don't worry. Now why don't you get back to bed and try to get some rest? If you need anything, just yell. I'll be right outside."

By the time they arrived, it was all over.

One of the choppers had spotted flames coming from the windows of the building and radioed one of the squads to investigate. It could have been merely another fire. It happened frequently in no-man's-land, with people building fires in the abandoned, derelict buildings in order to keep warm. The flames hadn't had much chance to spread, and the first squad on the scene managed to extinguish them with their portable fire-fighting gear. Then they called in to tell the other squads in the task force what they found. The other units rapidly converged upon the building.

Steele stepped into the charred and smoking apartment on the third floor. At some point, the walls had been knocked down so that it was a large room, opening out into the adjoining apartments on either side. The place was a wreck. Not that it must have looked like much to begin with. There was rubble on the scarred wooden floor, and the walls, where they weren't scorched, were covered with Chinese gang graffiti. A partially burnt flag with a green dragon on it and some Chinese characters hung limply on one wall. There was a makeshift bar and some battered old furniture scattered about. Some of it had burned. There were several crates placed around the walls. Most of them had either been opened or broken into.

One large, open crate was packed full of cocaine, which the Dragons had been rendering into crack. There were several metal garbage cans placed around the apartment in which fires had been built. Two of them had been knocked over, which had helped to start the fire, but it wasn't the only cause. There were bullet holes in the walls and in the battered furniture. And the walls were fire-scarred and cratered with what could only have been plasma blasts. And there was blood. A lot of blood. Spattered on the walls and furniture and ceiling, pooled and coagulating on the floor.

Volkirk turned toward Steele, his face pale and drawn. He looked ill. "Jesus Christ," he said. "Look at them."

Steele looked. And his stomach churned. The bodies had been hideously mutilated. The stench was awful. Huge chunks of them were missing, entire limbs chopped off, flesh cut from the bones as if they had been. . . .

"Butchered," Steele said.

"*Why*?" asked Volkirk. One of the other officers was doubled over against one of the walls, puking his guts out. "My God, why would he *do* this?"

"I don't think he did," said Steele.

"Then *who*?"

"Tunnel dwellers," Steele said grimly. "I've seen this sort of thing before. They didn't want to burden themselves with the bodies, so they just cut off the parts they wanted."

"Sweet Jesus," Volkirk said. "I've got to get some air."

They went outside. One of the officers approached them.

"Lieutenant, we found a survivor in the alley," he said. "Looks like he jumped from one of the windows. His legs are broken. He'd dragged himself into a pile of garbage. We would've missed him if he hadn't called out to us."

"I want to see him," Steele said.

They went back out to the street. The paramedics already had the surviving gang member on a stretcher and were about to load him into a waiting van.

"Wait," said Steele.

He came up to the stretcher and looked down at the Dragon. It was just a kid. Jason's age, maybe even younger. They all looked so tough and mean in their gang colors and their chains, with their studded bracelets and bandanas and their guns. But he didn't look so tough now. He just looked broken. They'd given him something for the pain, but he was still conscious.

"Can you talk?" said Steele.

"Yeah," the kid said dully.

"What happened?"

"Hell happened, man. He just came bustin' in, shootin'. Eyes glowin' with red lights. Him an' those goddamn tunnel freaks, lousy motherfuckin' cannibals. We never even had a chance. I went through a window. Broke my legs. Lucky. Others all got wasted."

"How many of them were there?"

"I dunno, man. Dozen, maybe more. Derelicts. Tunnel freaks. An' that red-eyed bastard. Fucker wasn't even human."

"What did they get out of those crates?" asked Steele.

"AKs. Vipers. Some M-14s and other stuff. Grenades."

"Grenades," said Steele. "Great. Just great." He glanced at the paramedics. "Okay, go ahead."

"Wait," said the kid. "You're Steele, aren't ya?"

"That's right. You know me?"

"Saw you on the news. You're just like him. That fuckin' red-eyed freak. He's another one like you, ain't he?"

The corner of Steele's mouth twitched. "Yeah. He's another one like me. Go on. Get him outta here."

They loaded the kid into the van.

"Don't let it get to you, Lieutenant," Volkirk said. "Stalker's not like you at all."

Steele's jaw muscles tensed. "Oh, yes he is, Volkirk. Yes, he is."

The three goons approached him as Ice came into the lobby of the building, his long black leather coat thrown over his shoulders like a cloak.

"Where d'ya think you're goin'?" one of them said. He drew back the bolt on his assault rifle.

Ice brought his hand up from beneath the coat and fired his big .44 magnum semiauto, shooting the goon right through the chest. As he flew backward, Ice quickly brought the gun around and shot the other one. The top of his head came apart in a spray of blood and bone. Ice snapped off a third shot, shooting the legs right out from under the third hired gun before he could bring up his weapon. The man went down, his rifle clattering to the lobby floor. He lay writhing on the ground, clutching his shattered kneecap, gasping and crying out with pain. It had all taken no more than about two seconds. Ice walked up to him and looked down at the writhing thug.

"No! No, Jesus, don't. . . ."

Ice stepped on his knee.

The scream tore through the lobby.

"Where's Rico?"

"*Ahhhh*! No, please. . . ."

Ice bore down again.

The man screamed with agony.

"Where?"

"*Ahhhh*! God! *God*! Top floor. . . . 12-A. Please . . . I need a doctor. . . ."

"No, you don't," said Ice. He raised his gun and shot the man through the head.

Though the building was just over the border inside no-man's-land, it still had power. Rico and the other residents could afford to pay their bills. Ice got into the elevator and punched the button for the 12th floor. As the elevator started to ascend, he glanced up and saw a security camera aimed down at him. He raised his gun and shot it. As the elevator reached the 12th floor, Ice stepped to the front and flattened himself against the wall, beside the sliding door. The elevator stopped and the door slid open. Immediately, an automatic rifle opened up, spraying the inside of the elevator. The instant the firing stopped, Ice stuck his arm around the door and fired. The shot took the man in the chest as he was trying to slap in a fresh magazine and hurled him back against the corridor wall. He slid down to the floor, leaving a smear of blood on the wall behind him.

Ice quickly glanced up and down the hall, then stepped out of the elevator, holding his gun ready. He bent down quickly and picked up the dead man's automatic rifle. An Uzi 9mm. carbine. He picked up the fresh magazine and slapped it in, then drew back the bolt. He hugged the wall as he moved down the corridor, heading toward suite 12–A. Everything was quiet. No one stuck their heads outside the doors. In this neighborhood, they knew better. He reached the door of 12–A and kicked it in, then quickly stepped back out of the way.

Three shots came through the open door. He crouched down low, stuck the barrel of the Uzi around the doorframe near the floor, and fired a short burst. He heard a cry and the sound of a body falling to the floor. He straightened up and took a quick, cautious glance inside. A man lay on the floor, gasping with pain and clutching at his bullet-riddled shins. The gun was on the floor beside him. He looked up, saw Ice and started to reach for the gun. Ice aimed the Uzi down at him.

"Don't even think about it," he said.

The man was breathing in short sobs. His legs were bleeding badly.

"Where's Rico?"

The man's mouth opened and closed spasmodically. He was in agony, starting to go into shock. Ice stood over him and aimed the Uzi right between his eyes.

"I ask you one more time," he said.

"Unnnh . . . Unnnnh . . . He's . . . not here. . . ."

"Where's Cory Steele?"

"Aaah . . . Jesus. . . ."

"*Where*?"

"She . . . she went with Rico . . . *Christ*. . . ."

"Where'd they go?"

"I . . . I dunno . . . I swear to God . . . uunnnh . . . I swear. . . ."

Ice decided the man was telling him the truth. He bent down and picked up the man's gun, then patted him down quickly. Aside from a knife, he was carrying no other weapons.

He quickly searched the apartment. One of the doors was locked from the inside. He stepped back and gave it a kick. It flew open. Several girls screamed. There were four of them, dressed in filmy nighties and lace lingerie, huddled together on the bed, clutching each other fearfully.

"Don't hurt us! Please! We'll do anything you want!"

"I'm looking for Cory Steele."

"Cory? She's not here."

"I know that. Where?"

"She went with Rico," one of the girls said. "He made a call, then took her with him."

"Who'd he call?"

"Somebody named Ricky B."

Ice frowned. "Rick Borodini?" he said.

"Yeah, that's right. He called him Mr. Borodini."

"*Damn*," said Ice through gritted teeth.

"Please . . . don't hurt us! We'll do anything!"

"Where'd he take her?"

"We don't know, mister. Honest, I swear to God. . . ."

"Shit," said Ice. "Stay here," he told the girls.

He went back out into the main room. The man on the floor was unconscious. He'd lost a lot of blood. Ice went over to the phone and picked it up, keeping his eye on the door. He quickly punched in the number. When the call was answered, he said, "This is Ice. Lemme talk to Hardesty."

He waited several minutes until the Strike Force chief's surly voice came on the phone.

"Hardesty," he said.

"I got a line on Cory Steele," Ice said. "Pimp name of Rico had her in his stable."

"Where are you?"

Ice gave Hardesty the address. "You better send some people down here. There be some bodies to clean up."

"I figured that," said Hardesty dryly. "Did you find Cory?"

"No," said Ice. "Girls here say Rico took her to see Rick Borodini."

"Christ," said Hardesty. "They'll use her to get at Steele. You know where Borodini is?"

"No, but Rico called him from this place. I figure I give you the number here, maybe you can find out where the call went."

"I'll get right on it. What's the number?"

Ice gave it to him.

"Okay, I've got it. Where are you going to be?"

"I wait here till your people show up, case Rico gets back first. Then I be back at Steele's place. I figure Rick be gettin' in touch. Call me there."

"Right. Can you describe the pimp?"

"Puerto Rican," Ice said. "Real pretty, long black hair with silver streaks, tall, slim, wears high heels, fancy clothes and lots of jewelry. Drives a old white Lincoln. You oughta have him on file. Last name's Calveri."

"Okay," said Hardesty. "I'll have a couple units out there

right away and I'll put out a bulletin on the car. And Ice . . . if this guy gets back before they get there, try not to kill him."

"Best tell your boys to hurry up then," Ice said.

He hung up the phone and went over to the bedroom door. The hookers were still huddling together on the bed, terrified.

"I be down in the lobby," he said. "If Rico call, you make like ain't nuthin' wrong, then come down and tell me. You do just like I say or I be *real* upset."

"Sure thing, mister. Anything you say."

He turned to leave.

"Hey, mister."

He turned back.

"You gonna kill him?"

"Yeah."

"Good," she said.

The white Lincoln pulled up in front of the old warehouse near the waterfront, just off Canal Street. Rico's driver, a knife-scarred, beefy former member of the Skulls, blew three short blasts on the horn and the door opened to admit them.

Men armed with automatic weapons quickly surrounded the car, and as Rico got out, they started searching it. Rick Borodini wasn't taking any chances. He had armed guards posted outside and on the roof as well. The place wasn't nearly as well fortified as the enclave in Cold Spring Harbor, but since the feds had raided it with Steele's help, the Borodini crime family had fallen on hard times.

Borodini's oldest son, Tommy, was dead. Shot by his own brother, Rico heard. Tommy B. had put the snatch on some government officials and was holding them for ransom, but the plan went sour when Steele hit the enclave and captured the old man. The feds had offered to cut a deal, to swap Victor and Paulie Borodini and their other prisoners for the hostages that Tommy and Rick had taken. But the word was that Tommy didn't want to deal. He had wanted to waste the hostages and take the whole operation for himself, write off his father and his brother. So Rick had shot him and cut the deal with the feds.

So far as Rico was concerned, it was no great loss. He had known Tommy Borodini well. He was part of Tommy's operation, and he had provided some special entertainment for him on a number of occasions. He'd never liked Tommy B., but he could understand him. Rick Borodini he didn't understand at all. Rick scared him. Tommy had been crazy, but Rick was totally controlled. He never showed a flicker of emotion. He was the coldest man that Rico had ever met.

The loss of the enclave had been a serious blow to Victor Borodini, but he was a long way from being finished. Though the Delanos had picked up a lot of his action, he still had people who were loyal to him and he still had powerful connections. He had a lot of money salted away and he maintained good relations with the Chingos and the Skulls. He still had politicians in his pocket who didn't dare to turn on him for fear of being exposed, and he was determined to put his operation back together. And Rico knew that when he got back on top, as he had no doubt that Borodini would, he'd remember those who helped him on the way. And *this*, figured Rico as he pushed Cory ahead of him, was one fine present to be bringing to the man.

They were escorted through the warehouse toward some offices in the back. One of their escorts knocked on the door, then opened it to admit them. There were several rough-looking men inside the dingy office. At the desk, Paulie Borodini sat behind a small computer, entering data. The desk was piled high with paperwork. The slight, youthful, girlish-looking Paulie looked out of place in this environment, with his long hair and delicate features. He didn't even look up as Rico entered. He was intent upon his work. Paulie, Rico knew, was the brains behind the Borodini operation, the one who kept the books and carefully monitored all transactions. He was a marked contrast to his brother, Rick, who looked like a male model, fit and darkly handsome, always dressed in exquisitely tailored suits. The two brothers could not have been more unalike. The fragile Paulie had an innocent, childlike quality about him. Rick was hard and feral. He exuded deadly menace, like a barracuda.

"I brought you a present," Rico said with an evil grin.

Paulie looked up briefly, then went back to his work.

Rick came around the desk and stood in front of Cory. He lifted her chin up gently and looked into her eyes.

"So this is Steele's daughter," he said softly.

"Would you believe it?" Rico said. "She just fell into my lap. A runaway, picked up by one of my people. Until today, I didn't even know who her daddy was. Where's Mr. B.?"

"My father?" Rick said, still looking at the girl. "You didn't think he would be *here*, did you?"

"Well, I don't know, I figured—"

"Don't figure," Rick snapped. "My father's somewhere safe, until we can establish a new and more permanent base of operations." He smiled at Cory. "And I think this young lady's going to help us do that. You can go," he said to Rico.

Rico hesitated.

"Was there something else?" asked Rick.

"Well . . . I'm gonna lose money on this girl," said Rico.

"You'll be taken care of," Rick said. "Paulie, give the man five large out of petty cash."

Paulie reached into one of the desk drawers and removed a cashbox. He took out five hundred dollars and handed it to Rick. Rick stuffed the money into Rico's inside coat pocket.

"Thanks, Mr. B.," said Rico, disappointed that it wasn't more. But he figured he had bought some good will as well.

"Show him out," said Rick.

As Rico walked out, Rick turned to one of the men seated in the office and nodded to him. The man got up and followed Rico out.

Rico was escorted back to his car. As the warehouse door was opened, the driver started up the Lincoln. Rico lit up a cigarette. Five hundred wasn't all that bad, he thought. She'd have brought in much more than that in a couple of days once he had her broken in right, but it was better than nothing. Besides, there were always more where she came from. He rolled down the window . . . and stared with disbelief at the silenced barrel of the 9mm. semiautomatic pointing at his face. The gun coughed twice. Rico slumped over in the seat.

The gunman holstered his weapon, then opened the car door and retrieved the five hundred-dollar bills from Rico's inside coat pocket. He turned and spoke to the driver.

"Take the car out and dump it somewhere," he said.

The man nodded without a word. He turned on the radio and slowly backed the Lincoln out through the doors. They closed behind him.

7

It was late by the time Steele's chopper landed on his penthouse helipad. There had been no further sign of Stalker. After hitting the Dragons, he had simply disappeared, most likely back into the warren of subway tunnels underneath the city. It would have been impossible to search them all. There were tunnels down there they didn't even know about, and with the acoustics down there, a body of men would make too much noise no matter how quietly they tried to move. The best they could do for now would be to patrol the old subway entrances and seal up as many of them as possible.

Steele left word to be summoned the moment Stalker was spotted again and went back to his penthouse when the shift changed. He wasn't physically tired and he didn't really need to sleep, though his mental engrams were psychologically conditioned to it. He felt emotionally drained, and he badly needed to know if any leads had been turned up in Cory's case.

He found Ice and Raven waiting for him. Jason was awake as well. He looked a little better, but his battered face looked tired and drawn. Poor kid, thought Steele. He's growing up hard and fast, before his time.

"Any luck?" asked Raven.

Steele shook his head. "No. He's still out there somewhere, laying low for now. What about you?"

"The news ain't good," said Ice.

"He found out where Cory was," said Raven.

"Was?" said Steele, tensing.

"Jason identified the pimp who beat him up," said Raven. "It was Rico."

"*Rico*?" Steele said. "Not that same psycho who turned you over to the Skulls?"

Raven nodded.

"Jesus Christ," Steele said. "I should have taken care of that bastard after what he did to you. Only I didn't, and now . . ."

"Don't blame yourself," said Raven. "You never had the chance. You had your hands full with the Borodinis. Anyway, it's all come back full circle."

"What do you mean? Where is she?"

"Rick Borodini's got her," she said.

Steele stared at them. He had a hollow feeling in the pit of his stomach, as if the bottom had dropped out of it.

"Rico used to be hooked up with Tommy B.," said Ice. "I went over there to get your little girl and found out he'd taken her to Rick. She musta told him who she be. I called Hardesty. He sent some people over there, but Rico never showed. We been waitin' here, figuring' Borodini would call with some kinda demand, but there ain't been no word."

Steele lowered himself into a chair and closed his eyes. "They're going to use her to get back at me."

"What do you mean?" said Jason with concern. "They're not going to hurt her?"

"I don't know," Steele said. He sounded dazed. He rubbed his forehead wearily. "If it was Tommy Borodini, I wouldn't put it past him, but Rick's different. I'm the one they want. He'll most likely use her for a bargaining chip."

The phone rang. Jason lunged for it.

"Steele residence," he said tensely.

"Jason? Is that you?"

"Yes. Chief Hardesty?"

"That's right. How're you feeling, kid?"

"Better, thanks. You want to talk to Dad?"

"Yeah, put him on."

Steele took the phone. "Jake? Any news?"

"Rico's car was found down in Times Square. He was inside, shot twice through the head. Looks like they took him out and dumped him so he couldn't let us know where the Borodinis are."

"At least we know they're somewhere in the city and not out on the Island," Steele said. "If they were out there, you never would've found him. Car turn up any clues?"

"Not so far," said Hardesty. "But we're checking it over just the same. Have you heard from Borodini?"

"Not yet."

"Well, this may be something. I checked on all calls going out from Rico's place. We've got one that sticks out like a sore thumb. Address down on Canal Street."

"That's in no-man's-land on the south end," said Steele.

"Yeah. Not too many phones down there. I've sent some units down to check it out."

"Give me the address, I'll meet them down there."

"I'd rather you stay put," said Hardesty. "Stalker is still out there somewhere. Let my people handle this."

"Dammit, Jake, we're talking about my daughter!"

"I know. And you should be there in case Borodini calls. Besides, we still don't know that Cory's down there. If she is, we'll get her. If not, I'll let you know right away."

Steele sighed. "All right. But for God's sake, tell them to be careful."

"They will. They know it's family. I better get off the phone. We've put a tracer on your line, just in case Borodini gets in touch. Try to keep him talking. I'll get back to you soon as I know anything."

"Okay, Jake. Thanks."

He hung up the phone.

"What is it?" Raven said.

"Rico's dead," said Steele. "They found his body in his car, abandoned in Times Square."

"Look like Ricky B. save me the trouble," Ice said.

"Rico called someplace down on Canal Street," Steele said. "Jake's sent some units down to check it out."

"I'll keep my fingers crossed," said Raven.

Steele glanced at his son. "Jason, have you called your mother?"

"No. I was waiting for Cory to get back."

"You'd better call her," said Steele. "I promised to let her know if either of you turned up. She's worried about you. You should let her know you're safe."

"She'll only want me to go back," said Jason.

"And that's exactly what you should do," Steele said.

Jason looked stung. "You don't want me here?"

"It isn't that, son. But your mother's got legal custody. I can't keep you here against her wishes. Besides, with things the way they are, I'd be much happier knowing you were safe with her."

"I'm not going back without Cory!"

"You'll do what I tell you!" Steele snapped.

It suddenly got very quiet in the room.

Steele sighed, regretting his outburst. He was under a lot of stress, but that was no reason to take it out on the kid. "Look, Jason, I—"

"You can send me back," said Jason defiantly, "but you can't make me stay. Cory needs me! I'm the one she always came to when things went wrong, because I was the one who was always there for her. She could never talk to Mom. Mom didn't want to hear about things going wrong. And most of the time, you just weren't there."

Steele winced.

"And when you *were* there, she could never talk to you, because of Mom. You think we didn't know what was going on? The two of you could hardly talk to one another without fighting," he said bitterly. "And then you'd try to make up with each other, only it would never last. And there was never any time for us. Not like it used to be. Oh, sure, there were the family get-togethers, like when we'd go to visit grandma, but the two of you were just going through the motions. It's like if it wasn't for us, the two of you would've split up long ago. You think we didn't know that? You think we didn't care?"

"Jason, you don't understand—"

"Don't I? Fine, then you explain it to me! You explain about all the times you didn't come home! Explain about the times the phone rang when you weren't around and one of us would pick it up and they'd hang up on us! Explain about the times Mom would pick up the phone and say she couldn't talk now! What did you think, that we were stupid? That we didn't see what was going on? All Cory and I ever had was each other! Maybe it wasn't all we ever wanted, but it was all we had. And now Cory's in a lot of trouble and *I'm* the one she called for help. If you won't let me stay here and help to get her back, I'll do it myself somehow. But I'm not going back without her!"

He was close to tears. To avoid breaking down in front of them, he went back into the bedroom and slammed the door.

Steele simply stood there, staring after him, still feeling the sting of the boy's words. "I guess I didn't handle that too well," he said.

"No, you didn't," Raven said quietly.

"Kid gotta lot of guts," said Ice. He turned to Steele. "Maybe Jason not a man yet, but he ain't no little boy, either. Ain't no use treatin' him like one." He got up. "I goin' down get me some shut-eye. Call me anything goes down."

Steele grimaced and went over to the bar to pour himself a drink. "You want one?" he asked Raven.

"Sure, why not?" she said.

"Sometimes I wish I was capable of getting drunk," he said, pouring their drinks. "I feel so goddamn *helpless*."

"You're doing all you can," she said.

"Maybe, but it's not enough. Not nearly enough." He sat down beside her. She moved closer to him. "They're good kids, Raven. They deserved a lot better than this. A *lot* better. It seems like anyone who gets near me winds up getting hurt."

"Blaming yourself's not going to help them," she said. "Very few people get what they deserve. Both good and bad. You play the cards you get and try to make the best of it."

"She's such a sweet kid," he said, his voice sounding hollow. "What's going to happen to her?"

"She'll get through it," Raven said. "If she's anything like her brother, or like her old man, she'll make it."

"I hope so," Steele said dully. "I pray to God she does. But she'll be scarred for life by this."

"I know," said Raven. "She'll need a lot of help. I wish there was something I could say to make you feel better, but words ain't gonna help. This is a very heavy scene. Still, for what it's worth, she'll probably be much better off with the Borodinis than with Rico."

"It's not worth much, but I suppose it's worth something," Steele said. "I'm glad that son of a bitch is dead. I only wish I'd been the one who killed him." He sighed. "On the other hand, if Rico was alive, we'd know where Cory is now."

The phone rang. Steele grabbed it up.

"Steele."

"It's Jake, Steele," said Hardesty.

"Did you find her?"

"Bad news, I'm afraid. We busted the warehouse, but Cory wasn't there. Neither were the Borodinis. We just got some small fry."

"But they know where Borodini is," said Steele. "I'll be right down. I'll make the bastards talk."

"Forget it," Hardesty said. "Their lawyers are already here. Besides, I don't think they know where Borodini is. We grilled 'em pretty good, but they're nothing but hired muscle. The old man is a cagey bastard. I doubt anyone besides Rick and Paulie and a few trusted soldiers who are with him know where he's hiding out. We've got some units stationed at the warehouse, just in case, but they won't be coming back. The news media sniffed the bust somehow and they've already blown the story."

"Goddamn reporters."

"Tell me about it. They've been on my ass about Stalker 'round the clock, especially that Tellerman woman. I've given them everything I know, but they're still convinced I'm holding out on them. And when your man Higgins found out I was talking to the press, he just about had a coronary. He threatened me with charges, but I told him that you'd autho- rized it. He wasn't very happy. The media's been on his ass as well. I haven't left the office since this whole thing started. I've been catching cat naps on a fucking cot. Have you heard anything from Ricky B.?"

"No, nothing," Steele said.

"How's the kid holding up?"

"He's under a lot of strain, but he's hanging tough," said Steele.

"Anything you want me to do?"

"No, I guess you've already done all you could," said Steele with resignation. "Any word of Stalker?"

"Nothing. I don't know if that's good or bad."

"Neither do I," said Steele.

"Steele, look, I . . ." Hardesty hesitated.

"What is it, Jake?"

"Look . . . what are the odds that Stalker might just . . . break down or something?"

"I don't know, Jake. I can't give you the odds on that any more than I can give you odds on whether or not I'll start malfunctioning. Stalker and I are both experimental prototypes. The only man who might've been able to answer that one was Dr. Phillip Gates, only he's dead."

"Yeah, well . . . I just figured I'd ask. He'd save us all a lot of trouble if he self-destructed somehow. But I guess that would only give you something new to worry about. I'm sorry, I shouldn't have brought it up."

"Forget about it. It'll probably get worse before it gets better."

"I'm afraid you're right. You holding up okay?"

"Yeah. I was designed to. Unfortunately, so was Stalker. Get some rest, Jake."

He hung up the phone.

"I better go look in on Jason," he said. "Tell him I'm sorry. Not that it's going to fix anything."

"It might," said Raven, smiling.

Steele opened the door of the guest bedroom. Jason was lying on the bed. He was fast asleep, but his face was still damp with the tracks of his tears. Steele stared at his son for a long moment, then softly closed the door.

• • •

Higgins had spent the night on the couch in his office. He was tired from lack of sleep, but when he checked, he found out that Jennifer Stone had already been working since five o'clock that morning. He debated going down to see her, then decided to leave word for her to stop by his office whenever she had a chance. The two of them needed to talk.

They hadn't spoken much afterward. In the aftermath of the passion that overcame them both, there had been an awkward embarrassment, with neither of them really quite knowing what to say. After all, they barely knew each other.

He spent most of the day coordinating with the agents he had sent out to assist the task force searching for Stalker, but they weren't making much progress. What they did have to report was hardly encouraging. Stalker had organized a bunch of savage derelicts and had hit one of the gangs, seizing a large cache of weapons. The media found out about it and they were having a field day with the story. CITY UNDER SIEGE! RENEGADE CYBORG ON THE LOOSE! AUTHORITIES HELPLESS! To make matters even worse, Chief Hardesty had been talking to the press. In direct disobedience to orders, Steele had authorized him to give out the information, on the theory that they'd need all the help they could get from an alert and informed citizenry.

Maybe he was right, Higgins thought with resignation. Steele had his own way of doing things. He was insubordinate as hell, but he always got results. And maybe it was better to cooperate with the media up front than have them get wind of it on their own and start screaming, "Cover up!" But the result was that Higgins had to spend most of the day doing a great deal of explaining to his superiors, who were being pressured by angry members of the legislature. There was talk of scuttling the project. Higgins spent most of the day on the phone, playing every card he had, but the most he could achieve was a compromise. They would put the project on indefinite hold. Which meant no more allocations from the committee, which meant no more budget, which meant that after this year's resources ran out, if the committee did not vote to continue with the project, the whole thing would be history.

And as if he didn't have enough problems, throughout the entire day, he had not been able to get Jennifer Stone out of his mind.

Nothing like that had ever happened to him before. Contrary to the old glamorous image of secret agents, Higgins had never been a playboy. He had always been very conservative and old fashioned when it came to personal relationships. In his line of work, he had to be. He had never become intimate with anyone he didn't know extremely well. He had a file on Jennifer Stone, but being thoroughly familiar with it was not the same as knowing her. And there were significant gaps in it when it came to her personal life. He sat in his office, looking over her file once more, as if there could be something in it that could help him understand what had occurred the previous night.

Since the war, intelligence gathering capabilities weren't what they used to be. In a well-organized society, intelligence gathering was vastly simplified, but they no longer lived in a well-organized society. The one they lived in was severely crippled. Many people's lives were no longer thoroughly documented. Consequently, there were limits to what even the CIA could learn. Outside the core cities, birth records were scarce or completely non-existent. Educational records were spotty, at best. Records of employment were not always available. Society was too busy trying to survive to bother keeping records. Where the government retained any semblance of control, there were such things as taxation and voter registration, personnel records and social services, school and hospital records and other things through which a person's life could be traced to at least some degree. But within a mere twenty-minute drive of where Higgins sat, there were the slums of no-man's-land, virtually lawless, with its own underground economy, such as it was. There wasn't any way of knowing how many people lived there, much less who they were or the details of their lives. It was the same in much of the rest of the country.

In Jennifer Stone's case, her file was more complete than most. Except for details of her personal life. That bothered Higgins. Everything about Jennifer Stone bothered him. The way she'd gotten to him bothered him especially. He was intensely attracted to her from the very first moment he set eyes on her, but he had not been prepared for the incredibly powerful surge of chemistry that had occurred between them. Even now, he wanted her so badly that he ached. And in the coldly rational part of his brain, alarms were going off all over the place. Control had always been of paramount importance to him. And now, for the first time, he had lost it. He had lost control of the project when Stalker ran amok, and now it seemed he was losing control of his personal life as well.

His secretary buzzed him.

"Dr. Stone to see you, sir."

"Send her in, please."

The door opened and Jennifer came in.

"You wanted to see me?"

"Yes, Jennifer, come in, please."

Belatedly, he realized that he still had her file on the desk in front of him. He closed it and put it away in his desk, but her eyes—or her intuition—were too quick for him.

"Is that my file?"

Higgins nodded.

"That's not really very fair, is it?" she said. "I know almost nothing about you."

"I know. Jennifer, please sit down."

She sat across the desk from him and crossed her extremely attractive legs. Higgins tried hard not to stare at them, but he could already feel his blood pressure rising rapidly.

"We need to talk," he said.

"Look, about last night . . ." she started. She blushed. "I just wanted you to know that—"

"Jennifer—"

"No, let me finish. This is . . . this isn't very easy for me. I mean, I don't even know if you're married or not."

"I'm not."

"Well . . . I'm glad to hear to that, anyway. I'd hate to think that I—"

"Jennifer, look—"

"I just wanted you to know that if what happened between us

is going to be a problem for you, I've already made out my resignation," she said quickly.

"You want to resign?" he asked, surprised.

"No, I don't *want* to resign," she said, "but I'm well aware that this is a sensitive situation, and we're both under a great deal of stress as it is without. . . ." She took a deep breath. "Without personal pressures getting in the way. So if it will make matters easier for me to leave, I will."

"I don't want you to leave," he said. "For one thing, you've got the perfect qualifications for this job, and it would be very difficult to replace you on such short notice. For another, I'd like very much for you to stay. For personal reasons." He paused. "I must admit that I wasn't prepared for what happened between us last night, but I want you to know I don't regret it for a moment. I've been thinking about it all day."

She moistened her lips nervously and looked down at the floor. "I don't know what came over me," she said. "I've never done anything like that before."

"Well, neither have I," said Higgins. "But I really don't see any reason for us to feel guilty or awkward about it. We're both consenting adults, for God's sake, and things like that happen. We've both been under a lot of stress, and in the excitement of everything that was—"

"You don't understand," she said. "What I meant was that I never . . . well, I never. . . ." She blushed and her voice trailed off. The cool, totally professional, efficient and unflappable Jennifer Stone suddenly seemed like an embarrassed schoolgirl.

For a moment, Higgins didn't understand what she was talking about, but then it dawned on him, and he stared at her with astonishment.

"You mean . . . are you seriously telling me you've never had a man before?"

She recovered some of her composure and looked him directly in the eyes. "You were the first," she said.

"I can't believe it. A woman like you? Haven't you ever been in love?"

"I've never had the time for it," she said. "Well . . . that's not entirely true. I didn't want to *make* the time. I've had plenty of opportunities, and there have been men I've felt attracted to, but I didn't want to complicate my life."

So that explained why there was nothing about her personal life in her dossier, thought Higgins. The lady was the ultimate workaholic. She didn't *have* a personal life.

"I'd set certain goals for myself," she continued, "and I didn't want anything to get in the way of my accomplishing them. I've observed that men tend to get in the way a lot. I'm not unaware of my looks. But when you look the way I do, men often don't take you very seriously. And I've got no room in my life for a man who won't take me seriously. I've basically never had room in my life for a man, period. My work means everything to me, Oliver. Ever since I was old enough to read and find out what the world was like before the war. These days, most people are content to just survive. Or to grab as much for themselves as they can. I've never been satisfied with that. I wanted to *change* things. I didn't want to end up married, with children, worrying about what kind of rotten world they were growing up in, not knowing what their chances would be. I wanted to *do* something about it. So I avoided personal relationships because they just didn't fit in."

"You threw yourself into your work instead," said Higgins.

"And I've never regretted it," she replied. "But after last night . . ." She sighed and shook her head. "I can easily intellectualize what happened last night. A new environment, different from anything that I've been used to, an exciting, challenging new job, the sort of thing I'd worked for all my life, an element of danger, the stress, the anxiety, the thrill of the discovery relating to that backup engram program, the adrenaline flow and being alone with you . . . and you're not by any means an unattractive man. I've been sublimating my sex drive all these years, a virgin at the age of thirty-four, and it all suddenly exploded. But understanding why it happened is one thing. The emotions that go with it are something else again."

"I know exactly what you mean," said Higgins.

"The intelligent and logical thing to do," she said, "since

you don't want me to resign and we're going to have to work together, is for us to accept what happened like mature adults and write it off to a brief fling and simply let it go at that."

Higgins pursed his lips and nodded. "Except there's just one problem," he said. "I don't know about you, but I guess I'm not feeling too intelligent and logical right now, because I don't really want to let it go at that."

Jennifer Stone took a deep breath and let it out in a long and heavy sigh. "Neither do I," she said. "I guess that means we've got a problem."

"It doesn't have to be one," Higgins said. "I think we're both professional enough not to let our personal feelings get in the way of what we have to do. And if it starts to become a problem, then I think we're both intelligent enough to admit it to ourselves and break it off with no hard feelings."

"It could get sticky," she said.

"I won't let it be, if you won't. Look, Jennifer, we don't really know each other very well, but we know we've got at least one thing in common. We're both married to our work. We should be able to respect that in each other."

"I'd like to think so," she said.

"Would you have dinner with me tonight?"

"I can't. The lab still isn't ready. I have to work." She smiled. "You see what I mean? I told you that personal relationships get in the way."

He grinned. "You have to eat."

"I usually have a sandwich sent down from the cafeteria."

"A drink after hours, then."

"We're already both working on too little sleep."

"We'll make it a short one. And you can have another look at Steele's backup program."

"That's a dirty trick," she said with a smile. "You know I'm dying to spend more time with it."

"Hey, I'm a spook," he said with a shrug. "We specialize in dirty tricks."

She sighed, defeated. "Okay. You win. I'll come up after I'm through for the day downstairs. But only on one condition."

"What's that?"

She grinned. "Can we use the couch this time? My back's still sore from that damn desk."

Stalker hadn't slept since he broke out of the project labs at the Federal Building. He wasn't tired. He was driven by a restless energy, and while his brutish followers camped down in the darkness, huddled around a fire they'd built on the tracks, Stalker roamed the abandoned tunnels, trying to make some sense of his existence. He did not recall being Mick Taylor. Mick Taylor's thoughts and memories flickered through his mind, like brief electronic discharges, but then got lost once more as bits and pieces of engrams from other personalities came flooding in to confuse him. He didn't know that something had gone disastrously wrong with the programming of his data engram matrix. All he knew was that his mind was in a turmoil. And he vaguely remembered having died.

His computer mind was a jumbled confusion of overlapping memories and experiences. There was no way he could understand what had happened to him. He did not know that his persona was a blend of Mick Taylor's identity, downloaded from his damaged brain, and what Dr. Gates had called "ancillary data," mental engrams recorded from other test subjects in the Project Download experiments. Somehow, something had gone wrong when the program had been assembled. Or perhaps the problem had occurred when the engram matrix had been loaded into his cybernetic brain. There was no way of knowing exactly what had triggered the malfunction. But somehow, the ancillary data engrams had become disassociated from the matrix and Stalker had become a paranoid, homicidal schizophrenic.

He continually relived fragments of his own and other lives. He could still feel the agony as he stumbled from the wreckage of the Strike Force pursuit vehicle, his body torn and bleeding, wreathed in flames, and then the second explosion came before he could get more than several steps away from the burning hulk. The force of the blast had picked him up and hurled him through the air. Hot shrapnel peppered him, slicing into his body and his brain, and the last thing he remembered thinking before he slipped away was, *"Steele."*

He knew that Steele had brought him to that place where it all happened. He knew that Steele had left him there to die. He did not remember that Steele had gone into the abandoned, crumbling storefront in no-man's-land to meet with Ice, a man with a contract on his life because he had resisted Victor Borodini's takeover of the Skulls. He did not remember that it was Borodini's hired assassins who had blown him up and rained fire into the abandoned storefront, shooting Steele down while their primary target escaped. In his twisted reasoning, he only knew that Steele was responsible for what had happened to him, and he believed that it was Steele's fault that he had come back from the dead, part human, part machine, tormented by a cybernetic brain whose programming had gone haywire.

A part of Stalker didn't want to live. He longed for sweet oblivion, a surcease from the constant confusion of images and memories that plagued him, images and memories that he could not reconcile. He heard voices talking to him, voices from a dim past that held no meaning for him. He could not shut them up. He didn't want to live like this. But another part of him was driven by a strong, relentless, fighter's urge for survival. He was being pulled in separate directions. Conflicting emotions raged within him like a firestorm.

He knew that they were hunting him, but that didn't worry him. He was able to monitor their every move. He had been designed with both broadcast and receiving capabilities and a scrambler circuit had been built into his brain, enabling him to instantly decode police and government transmissions. They didn't know he had that capability, and it was a simple matter for him to stay several steps ahead of them.

He had learned from monitoring the police transmissions that Steele's daughter had been kidnapped. By somebody named Borodini. He had a dim recollection of that name. He also had a vague memory of a young and pretty teenaged girl named Cory. The police were looking for her.

Perhaps he could find her first.

• • •

They had stayed up late, waiting, but there was still no word from Rick Borodini or his father. Raven finally went to sleep, but Steele didn't want to come to bed. He didn't want to sleep. Sleep would only bring the nightmares once again. Nightmares that could, he realized, be a grim harbinger of what could yet become of him. It frightened him to think that what had happened to Mick Taylor could occur to him. And if that was in the cards, there was nothing he could do about it.

He felt helpless in the face of what was happening. He didn't have a clue as to where Cory was. He thought of Janice and the anxiety and guilt she must be suffering, and in spite of all the hurt that she had brought him, his heart went out to her. And he thought of Mick, or the creature that had once been Mick, and the knowledge that there was nothing he could do to help his old friend and partner twisted in him like a knife. His orders were to neutralize him. To take him out. To kill him. He tried to tell himself that if their positions were reversed, he'd want Mick to do the same for him, but that thought didn't give him any comfort.

His thoughts returned to Cory. Would Borodini kill her to get back at him? If so, then she was undoubtedly dead already. But he didn't believe that Borodini would take his satisfaction so cheaply. Victor Borodini was not that kind of man. He was the kind of man who'd want his full pound of flesh. He would not kill Cory. She was too valuable a tool to use against his enemy.

By now, with the police bust of his warehouse, Borodini had to know that Steele knew he had his daughter. The son of a bitch is making me sweat, thought Steele. And with the news media going wild over the Stalker story, Borodini would know about that, too. He'd take full advantage of it. Only Steele did not know exactly how. Would he play a waiting game and see if Stalker did his work for him? Or would he wait for just the right moment to put the pressure on, forcing him to choose between his duty and his daughter?

One way or another, Steele thought, he had to act. He had to *do* something. He picked up the phone and called building security.

"This is Steele," he said. "I'm going out. I don't know when I'll be back, but I want to leave strict orders that neither Raven nor my son are to leave the building under any circumstances. Use reasonable force to detain them if necessary, but they are *not* to leave. I want to be sure that they'll be safe. Is that perfectly understood?"

"Yes, sir. I'll see to it that your instructions are passed on to all personnel."

"Thank you."

He hung up the phone, then went over to the arms locker and started to put on his battle gear. He was through playing a waiting game, waiting to hear from Borodini, waiting to see where Stalker would strike next. He'd take the fight to him. He had to be hiding somewhere underneath the city in the maze of subway tunnels. He'd search through every foot of them until he found him, no matter how long it took. And then he'd turn his attention to the Borodinis.

Assuming he survived.

8

Dr. Phillip Gates had pulled out all the stops in designing Stalker. With Steele, his first prototype, standing as living proof that a successful synthesis between a human being and a computer could be accomplished, he had thrown everything he had into Stalker, hoping to show the Finance Committee the true potential of such a synthesis. He had used VSLI technology in his design of the cybernetic brain, while in Steele's case, he had essentially limited himself to duplicating human brain function. But with Stalker, he had wanted to show what Very Large Scale Integration, hundreds of integrated circuits on a single chip, could really accomplish.

All Stalker had to do was find a telephone line he could tap into and use his vocal sythesizing capabilities to transmit a series of codes to the central telephone computers, thereby opening up and accessing the entire network. Once he had done that, an operation that took no more than a few seconds, Stalker was capable of monitoring every telephone conversation in the city. He did not consciously "listen" to every one of them. He didn't have to. All he had to do was key in certain specific words or phrases, such as "Steele," "Borodini," and "Cory." His computer brain could then "sweep" the telephone network at incredible speed, immediately focusing on and isolating any conversation in which those key words or phrases cropped up.

123

It was essentially the same technique used by the National Security Agency in the days before the Bio-War, when they listened in on the conversations of private citizens by sweeping the entire electro-magnetic spectrum. Once Stalker isolated a conversation in which those key words or phrases came up, he could then trace the call both ways in a matter of seconds. The police department did not have that capability. Only the CIA did, and Stalker had effectively disabled it when he wrecked their computer section in the project labs.

Monitoring police radio transmissions had given him the knowledge that Steele's daughter had been kidnapped by the Borodinis. Monitoring the telephone communications in the city gave him the knowledge of where Steele lived. Once he had the number, all he had to do was access the telephone company databanks for the address. So he listened patiently, monitoring Steele's phone line and continuing to sweep the network, waiting for a key word or phrase to be spoken. It came when he heard the words, "Mr. Borodini." His cybernetic brain immediately locked in on the conversation.

"Where are you calling from?"

"Don't worry, Mr. Borodini, there's no chance of a trace. I'm calling from my car phone."

Even as the man spoke, Stalker was already tracing the call.

"Okay, go ahead."

"We've been keeping Steele's place under surveillance, like you said. He just left the building. No chopper this time, he came out the front door."

"Is he in a police vehicle or on foot?"

"He's on foot. Looks like he's loaded for bear. He's got his full battle kit with him."

"All right. Follow him. But be careful. Don't let him spot you, no matter what you do."

"Hey, don't worry, Mr. Borodini. Ain't no way I want that nightmare comin' after me. We'll keep our distance, believe me. Shelly'll follow him on foot and I'll keep well back in the car."

"Good. See that you do. Keep me informed."

"You got it. By the way, how's our little houseguest doin'? She behavin' herself?"

"What's it to you?"

"I was just wonderin'. Y'know, that Cory's a fine lookin' little piece. When Dom and Johnny come to spell us, it might be nice if we could get better acquainted."

"You got short eyes, you know that, Gino?"

"Hey, c'mon, Mr. B. The girl's a hooker, for Christ's sake. I mean, it's not like she ain't spread 'em before. Where's the harm? Tommy woulda let us have a little party."

"You ain't workin' for Tommy now. You're workin' for me. Or maybe you ain't happy with that arrangement, Gino?"

"Hey, no, Mr. B., I got no complaints. I was only thinkin'—"

"Yeah, well get your mind outta your damn crotch and back on the job. That cock of yours is going to get you in a lot of trouble one of these days. What do you think Steele would do if he found out you'd boffed his daughter?"

"So what about all the guys she boffed while she was with Rico? Or maybe you just want her for yourself, huh?"

"Rico's dead, Gino. Maybe you wanna join him?"

"Okay, okay, forget I mentioned it. I didn't mean no offense."

"Just make sure you don't lose Steele. You're gettin' paid enough to take care of your kicks on your own time."

"Okay, I get the message."

"Good. Make sure you understand it."

Rick Borodini hung up.

And Stalker had the address where they were holding Cory.

Dev Cooper was no longer bothering to report to work at the project headquarters. The first day, he had called in sick. The second day, he didn't even bother calling. He didn't bother to shave, or wash, or change his clothes or even eat. He didn't bother to leave his apartment. He looked like hell and he was starting to stink. He didn't care. He had stocked up on booze, which he used to drink himself unconscious, and he had stocked up on pills, which he used to charge himself up in the morning and keep going through the day. The abuse was taking its toll.

Dev knew he was in trouble, but he no longer cared. He was wired, subject to violent mood swings, from energetic pill-induced euphoria to black depression. He was losing weight, his nerves were shot and his hands were almost always trembling. He couldn't even hold a cigarette steady, and his fingers were becoming nicotine stained from constant smoking. He was on the verge of a collapse.

He knew that nothing could be as emotionally devastating as unrelenting guilt. Guilt could do savage things to a man. Or a woman. No one was immune, except perhaps a sociopath, the most dangerous sort of psychological abnormality, because a sociopath wasn't really capable of human feeling. Dev Cooper was no sociopath. Far from it. He was on the extreme opposite end of the psychological spectrum. He was an empath, someone who felt too much, who cared too much, who could all too easily put himself in someone else's shoes. Especially if that someone else was hurting.

It was what had led him to become a psychiatrist. He truly cared about people. Their suffering became his suffering. When their hearts were breaking, his broke too. It was his empathy that made him so good at what he did. Their pain became his pain. He could get down with them and feel it, share it with them, draw it out of them and make it easier to bear. It was the most hazardous kind of psychotherapy, the kind that involved a heavy investment of emotion, and among those who practiced it, the mortality rate was frighteningly high. The therapist-as-Christ-figure was a dangerous game to play, and Dev's number had finally come up. He had always told himself that he was strong, but he wasn't strong enough for this.

How could he help a personality without a body? How could he give therapy to a human soul locked up in a computer program? How could he deal with a patient who was human, and yet at the same time, not human? And, most of all, how could he reconcile his own role in all of it, the fact that in having asked Gates to run off a copy of Steele's engram matrix and bringing it on line, he had participated in the creation of his own patient, an electronic clone? He had literally played God with a man's soul. And now that soul was holding him responsible.

Strong as he was, it was a burden that Dev Cooper could not bear. And there was no one who could help him shoulder it. He knew that Higgins had pulled another copy off his own backup file, which now meant that there were *two* of them, which only served to make things even worse. He had tried explaining it to Higgins, but Higgins didn't really seem to understand. He understood it well enough from a purely intellectual standpoint, but it had never really sank in to gut level. He didn't *feel* it. Perhaps he couldn't, for much the same reason most people could pass a pathetic derelict lying huddled in an alcoholic stupor on the street and never even see him. It was a reality they didn't want to deal with, because to accept it meant to accept responsibility for it. To let the feelings in. Dev Cooper couldn't keep the feelings out.

And the worst part of it all, what made it truly unbearable, was the fact that the program seemed to empathize with *him*. Which shouldn't have surprised him, because the program was Steele, his mental engrams, his identity, and Steele was not an insensitive man. Consequently, his backup program was not insensitive. Perhaps it could not see the wreck that Dev Cooper had become, because it had no eyes to see with, but it was wired to hear, and it could analyze the stress factors in his voice, hear his breathing and his heartbeat, listen to the incessant lighting of cigarettes and know that he was smoking too much, hear the sounds of a bottle being opened and listen to the swallowing noises and the slurring in his speech and know that he was drinking like a fish . . . he could hide nothing from it. He couldn't lie to it, he couldn't even avoid the necessity of lying by not answering its questions, because it could measure his heartbeat and respiration and draw its inferences from those.

Besides, Dev simply didn't have it in him anymore to continue trying to deceive it. It *knew*. And so he finally broke down and told it everything. He had intended to use the backup program as a therapeutic tool in getting to the bottom of Steele's problems, especially the nightmares caused by the cybernetic ghosts within his engram matrix, but instead the tables had become turned along the way. He and the matrix had experienced a role reversal. It was as if *he* was the patient now and the matrix was the therapist. And while Steele was certainly no psychiatrist, his years as a cop had given him a deep, gut-level understanding of what made people tick, particularly people who found themselves in trouble. Dev had become a drug-dependent alcoholic. Steele had met a lot of those. It was something he could understand.

"You've got to get a hold of yourself, Dev," the matrix said, with Steele's voice coming from the speaker of the VS peripheral. *"Stop punishing yourself. It's not really your fault."*

"Yeah?" slurred Dev, rising from his chair unsteadily. "Whose fault is it, then?"

"It's not a matter of blame," the matrix said. *"I'm certainly not blaming you. I understand that you had the best intentions."*

"Isn't that what the road to Hell is paved with?" Dev said, staggering over to the table and picking up the bottle of whiskey. It was almost empty. He chugged it down without bothering to use a glass and picked up a pack of cigarettes. He lit one with a trembling hand. The room was starting to spin. He steadied himself against the table.

"You need help, Dev. You're out of control."

"The whole fucking world is out of control," said Dev, stumbling over to the couch and sagging down upon it. He felt very dizzy. His head was throbbing. His mouth was dry. He covered his eyes with his arm and leaned back, coughing raggedly.

"You'll be in no shape to help anybody if you keep doing this to yourself. Wallowing in guilt and self-pity won't accomplish anything. Call Higgins, for God's sake. Don't be ashamed to ask for help."

"Help?" said Dev faintly. "From Higgins? That's rich."

"Then call a doctor."

"I can't. Security . . ."

"To hell with security. You're no use to anyone the way you are. You keep going like this and you'll give yourself a heart attack."

"Promises, promises . . ."

"Dev, snap out of it, God damn it! Stop torturing yourself! It won't solve anything. I don't need you like this!"

Dev's mouth dropped open and he began to breathe heavily.

"Dev?"

There was no response.

"God damn it, Dev . . ."

Dev Cooper started snoring.

"Dev! Wake up!"

Nothing.

"Dev!"

He was dead to the world.

"Shit!"

For a moment, nothing happened. The computer video display continued to glow softly, the word "shit" repeating itself over and over on the screen. Then it faded out. A moment later, the sound system came on. Dev had an old rock disc inside the system and the sound suddenly blasted through the apartment, but Dev remained totally oblivious to it. The lights started to flick on and off rapidly, like a strobe. And then the television set came on. It made no difference. Dev had crashed completely.

Linda Tellerman's face appeared on the television screen. Abruptly, the lights stopped flashing on and off and the sound system shut down. The TV remained on as the reporter continued to speak.

". . . force has made no further progress in the massive, city-wide manhunt for the renegade cyborg killer known as Stalker," Linda Tellerman was saying. "The latest word we have is that Stalker has apparently recruited an unknown number of heavily armed homicidal derelicts, and after assaulting the gang headquarters of the Green Dragons, Stalker and his followers have disappeared from sight, most likely taking refuge somewhere in the subway tunnels underneath the city. It is still unknown what the killer cyborg's capabilities are. Oliver Higgins, the director of the highly controversial project, could not be reached for comment, but we've had reliable reports that this new-generation cyborg is armed with state-of-the-art, built-in laser and plasma weapons systems. Earlier today, I spoke with Chief Jacob Hardesty of the Strike Force concerning police efforts to track down this deadly and relentless killer."

The camera cut to a tape of Jake Hardesty being interviewed at police headquarters. He looked utterly exhausted.

"Chief, Hardesty," said Linda, "exactly what is the status of the manhunt at this time?"

"We're doing everything we can," said Hardesty wearily. "We've got choppers covering the city and the entire Strike Force has been mobilized. We're also getting some help from federal agents, but the trouble is, we can't be everywhere at once. We'll get him, though. It's only a matter of time."

"Only how *much* time?" Linda said. "Isn't it true that up to this point, Stalker has outwitted the entire task force? The one time he was spotted and your officers gave chase, he annihilated the entire unit. What happens if he *can't* be stopped?"

"I don't deal in 'what ifs,' Miss Tellerman," said Hardesty. "I won't deny that Stalker is a formidable threat, but he's not indestructible. Nothing is."

"What about Lt. Steele? How does he feel about this? We haven't been able to get any comment from him."

"Lt. Steele is extremely busy. He's in charge of the task force. And if anyone is capable of stopping Stalker, Steele certainly is."

"Only if Stalker is a new-generation cyborg," Tellerman said, "doesn't that mean he's more advanced than Steele? Have you any comment on that?"

"I have no details on Stalker's engineering," Hardesty said.

"But it's true that he's equipped with laser and plasma weapons systems?"

"I'm not going to speculate on that," said Hardesty. "The important thing to know is that Stalker is extremely dangerous. He's experienced a serious malfunction and he's out of control.

Citizens should exercise extreme caution and stay off the streets. And if anybody out there spots him, call the task force command at once. We have several hot lines set up and they'll be manned twenty-four hours a day. But I cannot stress this enough. If Stalker is spotted, avoid contact at all costs and call the hot line *immediately*."

The camera cut back to Linda Tellerman in the newsroom. Behind her was a graphic slide, a photograph of officer Mick Taylor.

"Police have provided us with this photograph of Stalker," she said, "who was once officer Mick Taylor of the Strike Force division, before he was critically injured in an explosion that took place during a shoot-out with soldiers of the Borodini family. Ironically, it was during that same shoot-out that Lt. Donvan Steele was injured and later transformed into a cyborg. To compound the irony, officer Mick Taylor was Lt. Steele's partner on the force, and Steele now has the unenviable task of heading up the manhunt for the man who was once his partner and his friend. We cannot help but wonder what effect all this has had on him, especially knowing that a cyborg like himself, allegedly an updated, more advanced model, has suffered a malfunction of its cybernetic brain, rendering it a psychopathic killer. How can he help but wonder if the same thing couldn't happen to him? In the meantime, this crisis has resulted in the entire program being called into question. For more on that aspect of the story, we go to Ron Stevens, standing by at the Federal Building—"

The TV set suddenly winked off. For a long moment, the apartment was entirely silent, illuminated only by the glow from the computer screen.

Then the small red light on the telephone modem came on.

From the outside, it looked no different from the other rundown, crumbling buildings in the area once known as Soho, on the south end of Manhattan. Deep in no-man's-land, the building had four stories, the first and second of which, in the years prior to the Bio-War, had been an art gallery. The third and fourth floors were lofts, accessible from a separate entrance by a narrow flight of stairs or a large freight elevator. The large, one-room dwellings were numerous on the lower end of Manhattan, and they had once held various commercial and small industrial concerns. But as artists had started moving into Soho in the years prior to the war, these cavernous, brick-walled spaces had been converted into studios and large apartments for the city's young, upwardly mobile professionals.

Luxurious bathrooms and kitchens were installed and the old wood floors were painstakingly refinished. The cavernous spaces were filled with designer furniture, artistic room dividers, sculptures, mobiles, wall hangings and paintings, state-of-the-art sound and entertainment systems suitable for nightclub-sized parties and chrome and steel track lighting. The once rundown area became a chic New York City neighborhood, home to artists, literary types and pseudo-intellectuals who dressed down fashionably and drove the prices up in the seedy local bars and restaurants that were suddenly transformed into watering holes for the city's cultural elite.

Now, the elite of Soho were the Chingos, the largest and most powerful street gang on the south end of Manhattan. The Chingos membership was largely Hispanic, with a heavy ethnic mix, but not a single black. The dictates of a downtrodden social group in a fragmented society demanded that there be someone to look down upon, a common enemy, and in the Chingo's case, that enemy was black. It was also white, but only that polished shade of white that lived in Midtown.

Victor Borodini might easily have been perceived as such an enemy, except that he shared an ethic of power and survival with the Chingos that they could respect and understand. Like themselves, he was an outsider, a man who was wanted by the government, which increased his standing immeasurably. Like the Chingos, he had built his power base from scratch out in the wilds of Long Island. He was answerable to no one but himself. He had taken control of his own destiny, carving out an empire with coercion, violence and strength.

That he had lost much of this empire did not diminish his

stature in their eyes. The Chingos had suffered setbacks of their own in wars with other street gangs and in armed confrontations with police. They understood defeat and did not regard it as ignoble. What was ignoble to them was capitulation, but Victor Borodini had not done that. The feds had dealt him and his organization a crushing blow when they had seized his enclave, and further setbacks came when the Delano family had moved in on many of his operations, but Victor Borodini had not given up. He acted, in fact, as if nothing of significance had changed. He had merely rolled the dice and lost a bundle, but the game continued, and he still had stakes with which to gamble. He was a player and a fighter. A man worthy of respect.

The Skulls had deserted him, but the Chingos stuck. And Borodini saw to it that their loyalty was suitably rewarded. His operation was too multi-faceted to be shut down completely by the seizure of his enclave and the power grabs of the Delanos. He still had reserves the feds knew nothing of; he still maintained connections with the freebooters, who would gladly deal with both him and the Delanos, since they didn't deal in loyalties, only in hard cash. Victor Borodini might have been knocked down off his pedestal, but he was still a man of means and powers. His fingers were still on the pulse of the underground economy in the south end of Manhattan. He would rebuild his empire, and one day, as he had promised, he would control the entire city. When that day came, as the Chingos were convinced it would, they would be the honored frontline troops, the praetorian guard who had never left their Caesar. They protected him as worker bees would protect their queen. He was their royalty, the man who gave them standing in their blighted world.

From the outside, there was nothing about the building where Victor Borodini now resided that would attract anyone's attention. Inside, it was a different story.

It would have taken a full-scale armed assault to penetrate his defenses. There were guardposts inside the surrounding buildings and on the rooftops, manned with para-military precision by the Chingos. The main floor, on the street level, was a warehouse. The heavily reinforced steel shutters were soiled and dented and covered with graffiti, but they concealed a concrete bunker studded with gunports for automatic weapons and machinegun emplacements. The second story housed Victor Borodini's soldiers, a core group of his most loyal assassins, along with an extensive armory. The third floor was the operations center, from which Paulie and Rick Borodini ran the remnants of the Borodini empire, and the top floor was Victor Borodini's living quarters, a loft as elegantly appointed as any during Soho's heyday as a chic cultural community.

The freight elevator shaft went down to the basement, which had a hidden passageway leading to a section of abandoned subway tunnel. With his soldiers providing protection from the tunnel dwellers, Borodini could use it to come up in another part of the city or take it to the waterfront on the Lower East Side, where a boat was concealed for escape to the eastern end of Long Island. Victor Borodini had already made arrangements with the Brood for a safehouse near Mastic Beach, on the shore overlooking Moriches Bay. But though he had made all the necessary preparations, he wasn't planning on escape. He was planning on revenge.

He could scarcely believe the good fortune that had brought him Cory Steele. The daughter of his greatest enemy. He had known that Steele had family, but he had not known where they were. He had learned that after their divorce, Steele's wife had left the city with their two children, but none of his informants had been able to provide him with their location. And now the girl had simply fallen right into his lap. A runaway. A hooker. It was too delicious to be true. And the timing could not have been more perfect.

He gave strict orders that she wasn't to be touched. Then after Rick had brought her to him, he had installed her in his own private quarters and treated her with kindness and respect. After what she had been through, this new development confused her. Victor Borodini exploited that confusion.

He had seen to it that she had new clothes, jeans and sweatshirts, the sort of comfortable clothes that a teenaged girl would wear around the house, instead of the blatantly sexy hooker outfit that she had arrived in. He saw to it that she lacked for nothing, except the freedom to come and go as she pleased. And even on that point, he acted not so much like a jailer, but like a protector, treating her in a courteous and avuncular manner. It made for an effective form of control.

After Rico, she expected to be brutalized and used. After what she'd done, she had come to feel that she deserved it. It was a common form of Pavlovian conditioning, often used by pimps like Rico to break down their new girls. Make them feel powerless and worthless, destroy their self-esteem, if they had any to begin with. The pimp would replace their egos with his own and become God in their microcosmic world. After a while, often a surprisingly short while, the conditioning took hold, and they became like servile dogs, crawling back to lick their master's hand after he had administered a beating.

Rico had turned Cory Steele's whole world upside down, and now she'd had the rug yanked out from under her again. She was lost and frightened and confused. Reality had broken down for her, and she was ready to accept any substitute he offered.

"Are you feeling any better?" Borodini asked her kindly.

"A little," she replied uncertainly, desperately anxious to give the proper response.

"Good," said Borodini, smiling. Then he allowed his smile to fade. "I'm afraid we still haven't had much luck in finding your brother, Jason. I've got my people out looking for him, but . . ." he shrugged, as if with helpless frustration, ". . . it's a big city. And a dangerous one, too. As you have, unfortunately, discovered for yourself. Perhaps Jason gave up and went home."

"No," she said, shaking her head. "Jason would never give up on me."

But she didn't sound convinced.

Borodini sighed. "You realize, of course, there could be another possibility. From what you tell me, he sounds like a determined young man. Rico had already hurt him once. If Jason came back, then . . . well, it's possible that Rico might have . . ." He left the thought unfinished.

Her eyes widened in alarm. "No! No, please, you've got to help him! Find him! Don't let Rico hurt Jason!"

"Well, as you've already seen, I'm not without some influence," said Borodini, not bothering to tell her that Rico wouldn't be hurting anyone anymore. "I've made certain Rico understands that if anything happens to your brother, he'll have me to answer to. And I've told him that if Jason should come back, he's to bring him here to us at once. But like I told you, it's a big city and a dangerous one, especially for a young man like Jason, out there all alone . . ."

"Maybe . . . maybe Jason's with my daddy," Cory said hopefully.

"I'm afraid not," Borodini said. He sat down on the edge of her bed. "You see, Cory, there's something you need to know about your father." He hesitated, as if struggling with the decision.

"What? What about my father? He's all right, isn't he?"

"Well . . . in a way, I suppose you could say that he's all right. And in another way . . . I don't know, Cory. You've been through so much. I want to help you. But I don't want to cause you any more pain."

"*What*? What *is* it? Tell me, please!"

Borodini took a deep breath and let it out slowly, then he picked up her hand and held it gently in his.

"I don't quite know how to say this, Cory, but you see, your daddy's not really your daddy anymore."

"I don't understand. What are you saying?"

"You remember how you told me what your mother said to you when you left town? That your daddy had been killed?"

"She lied! I saw Daddy on the news!"

"Yes, I know you did," said Borodini gently. "Or at least, you *thought* you did."

"But I *saw* him!"

"Yes, I know you think you saw him, but what you saw wasn't really your daddy. You see, Cory, your mother told the truth. Your daddy *was* killed. But they used his body to make a sort of robot out of him. He still looks like your daddy, and he might even sound like your daddy, but he isn't. Not anymore."

She stared at him, looking dazed and frightened. "No! No, he can't be . . ."

"I'm afraid it's true, Cory. You remember what they called him on the news? A cyborg. That's short for cybernetic organism. A robot made from a man's body. That's why your mother left, Cory. She understood what they had done to him and she simply couldn't bear it. She knew that he wasn't really your father anymore. He probably doesn't even remember you and Jason. He's not a man anymore, Cory. He's a machine."

She began to cry.

"There, there," he said, pulling her close and stroking her hair. "You poor kid. It's so unfair."

"Oh, God," she wailed miserably, "what am I going to do? What's going to happen to me now? I can't go home, not after what I did. Oh, Mr. Borodini, can't you help me? I feel so awful! I'm so ashamed . . ."

"It's not your fault," said Borodini kindly patting her hand. "And I'm sure your mother would understand."

"No, she wouldn't! You don't know her! She'd never want anything to do with me again!"

"I'm sure that isn't true," said Borodini soothingly. "Look, why don't you let me call her? Tell me what the number is. Tell me where she lives. I'm sure I could explain it to her to that—"

"*No*!" she said, pulling away violently.

Borodini backed off. "All right," he said. "We've been over this before and I promised I wouldn't do anything you didn't want me to do. I'm only trying to help you, Cory, but if you don't trust me . . ."

"It's isn't that," she said. "I'm sorry. You've been very good to me, Mr. Borodini. And I'm very grateful, but I can't have you tell my mother, I just *can't*!"

"All right, fine, I understand how you feel. And I didn't want to upset you. Maybe you're right. Sometimes mothers don't really understand their daughters. But *I* understand, Cory, and we'll—"

Suddenly, the entire building shook.

Borodini stiffened.

"What is it?" Cory cried, frightened. "What's happening?"

"I don't know," said Borodini, "but I'll find out. Don't worry, whatever it is, we'll be safe here."

But even as he said it, he heard the muffled sound of gunfire from below. And it wasn't coming from outside, but from somewhere *inside* the building.

"Mr. Borodini, I'm scared!" cried Cory.

He rushed to the phone and snatched it up, stabbing at the intercom button. "Rick! What's going on down there? Rick? *Rick!*"

The door to his apartment suddenly flew open and Rick was there, along with Paulie and several of their men. They had come running up the stairs from the third floor. Rick and the others were all carrying weapons, all except for Paulie, who had never been much good with guns.

"Rick! What the hell is—"

"Someone's broken through the tunnel entrance in the basement," Rick interrupted. "Come on, we've got to get you out of here before they can take the elevator up to—"

But even as he spoke, the elevator doors slid open.

Rick and the others spun around, bringing up their guns, but they weren't fast enough. Stalker opened up on them with two AK-47s, one held in each hand. Cory screamed and Borodini stared in horror as his two sons and the men with them jerked like marionettes and fell, mowed down by the 7.62 x 39mm. jacketed slugs.

Borodini screamed with wounded rage and clawed for the pistol in his shoulder holster. He fired six times, rapidly, the bullets striking Stalker in the chest but with no apparent effect. The cyborg swung one of the AKs around and squeezed off a short burst. Borodini was hurled backward by the impact of the bullets on his chest. The flak vest he wore beneath his shirt had saved him, but he knew better than to move or make a sound. His ribs felt broken, but he gritted his teeth against the pain. Out of the corner of his eye, he saw Rick's hand twitch. He heard Paulie groan. He thanked God he'd made them wear their vests.

There was shouting and the sound of footsteps running up the stairs. Stalker slung one of his rifles and moved to the apartment door, pulling a grenade from his belt. He yanked the pin, held it for a moment, then lobbed it down the stairwell.

"*Jesus Christ!*"

"*Look out!*"

The incendiary grenade went off with a concussive roar, punctuated by the sound of screams. A wash of flame swept up and down the stairs.

Stalker closed the door and turned to the terrified girl.

"Cory, come with me."

She stared at him with disbelief, recognition dawning.

"Uncle Mick?"

He gazed at her, frowning faintly. *Uncle Mick*. The name touched a chord of memory.

Cory ran to her father's old partner, the man who'd held her on his knee when she was little, the man who always had a joke for her and an easy smile, who always told her how pretty she was and how grown-up she was looking. In a maelstrom of shock and confusion, she ran to the familiar, not knowing what she was really running to. Sobbing, she threw her arms around his neck. He put his arm around her waist and easily lifted her up off the floor, then stepped back into the elevator.

The doors closed and it started to descend.

Borodini rose to his hands and knees and started crawling toward his sons.

_9_

Whoever he was, he was good. Steele didn't pick him up until he was several blocks away from his building. He might not have picked him up at all if his amplified hearing had not alerted him to the sound of the man's footsteps following him.

It was late and the streets were deserted. Even in Midtown, people knew better than to chance going out at this hour of the night unless it was absolutely necessary. The occasional cab passed by as he walked purposefully toward Lower Manhattan, and once a police cruiser drove by slowly, stopping to investigate the man walking down the street carrying a 4.3mm. caseless battle rifle, but when they saw his Strike Force fatigues and recognized him, they relaxed, conferred with him briefly and drove on.

There had been no further sightings of Stalker, and Steele carried a portable radio tuned to the police band, just in case. The choppers were out patrolling overhead, and at least for now, everything was relatively quiet.

He had purposely chosen to come out and head down into no-man's-land on street level, rather than take a chopper or a car. He wanted to make himself a target. If not for Stalker, then for anyone, any hapless mugger whose path he might happen to cross. The fury and frustration that he felt needed an outlet. He wanted to strike out. At somebody. Anybody.

He had gone about eight blocks when he became aware that he was being followed. On this quiet night, with nothing but the distant sounds of chopper blades or sirens to break up the tense stillness of the city, he was easily able to pick out the sounds of footsteps coming from about a block or so behind him.

Whoever it was, he was being careful. It could be a mugger, Steele thought, but it would have to be a pretty desperate mugger, or a crazy one, to risk going up against a man carrying an assault rifle in plain view. But it was possible. There were some stone cold crazies who came out of their holes at night. Some of them would easily risk it for the chance of gaining the rifle. And though Steele was wearing the black Strike Force fatigues, he was not wearing the battle helmet or the backpack with its built-in computer and rocket launchers. So whoever was stalking him might not realize he was a cop. Either that, or his pursuer was so hardcore that he didn't care.

Steele wondered if it could be Stalker on his tail. He hoped it was. He was anxious to get the inevitable confrontation over with. His address was certainly no secret, thanks largely to the media, and Stalker could easily have found out where he lived. That had been one of his chief concerns right from the beginning. However, his building was well guarded by crack federal personnel and equipped with sophisticated, automated defense systems. Jason and Raven were as safe there as they would be anywhere, which was why he had left strict orders that they not be allowed to leave under any circumstances. So long as Stalker was on the loose, they were in danger.

What worried him the most was Stalker's recent inactivity. He had broken out of the project labs like gangbusters, taken on a Strike Force squad in order to get their weapons, gathered a band of bloodthirsty tunnel dwellers and wiped out most of the Green Dragons in a raid to seize their ordnance and then . . . nothing. He had simply disappeared from sight. *Why*? He had to be planning something. Only what?

Steele knew that Higgins had been badgering Hardesty to send units down into the tunnels in an effort to flush Stalker out, but Hardesty, wisely, had resisted. For Higgins, the priority was simple. Find Stalker and neutralize him. Save the project. For Hardesty, the issue was a great deal more complex. He not only had to worry about finding and neutralizing Stalker, he had to worry about the safety of the city's populace as well. He did not want to risk taking units off patrol and sending them down into the tunnels, where they would be unable to respond quickly if Stalker and his derelict army struck in the streets above. Higgins might have pressed the issue harder, bringing federal authority to bear, but he was hesitant to do so with the media in full roar. Higgins realized that if Stalker struck and citizens of Midtown died, Hardesty could claim that there hadn't been a quick enough response because Higgins had ordered him to send his units down into the tunnels, and the media would then place responsibility squarely on his shoulders.

The media had once been behind the project all the way, especially with Linda Tellerman doing the cheerleading. After Steele's part in the seizure of the Borodini enclave, she had undertaken that role, though not out of a belief in Steele and what the project had accomplished, but because her bottom line was ratings. With Steele regarded as a hero, she had quickly hitched her wagon to his rapidly ascending star. With Stalker, she had changed her tune.

Now, she was saying that the government was being irresponsible, endangering the people, pushing the new technology too fast and not observing proper safeguards, with the result that a killer cyborg had been unleashed upon a helpless city. And she saw no inconsistency in the change of her position. In her nightly reports, she was careful not to lump Steele in with Stalker as a menace to the city. Instead, she cast him in the role of victim, a pawn of an uncaring government bureaucracy that was now using him to make up for its mistakes. Steele and the police were still the heroes. The government and its "irresponsible, uncaring technocrats" were villains. And the only ones who won in such a situation were Linda Tellerman and the other media hounds who had taken up her battle cry.

Personally, Steele cared nothing for the project. The last

thing he wished to see was more men transformed into cyborgs like himself. He would not wish that on anyone, least of all the man who'd been his partner and best friend. Still, he had his duty to perform, no matter how he felt about it, and the media weren't making things any easier. But there was no avoiding it. It would have been far worse if he had done as Higgins wanted and tried to keep the lid clamped down. The task would have been impossible. They would have found out anyway, and keeping them out of the loop would only have served to fuel their fire. And no matter how the end result turned out, Steele knew that he could only lose. Stalker was planning something. And whatever it was, Steele had to find him before he could carry it out.

However, before he could do that, there was the matter of the tail he had picked up.

Steele turned a corner and ducked into the shadows of a storefront entrance. He did not have long to wait. In a few moments, the man came around the corner. But he was being cautious. The instant that he realized he had lost sight of Steele, he stopped, hesitating.

Steele could hear his breathing. He could hear the increase in his heartbeat. The man suddenly realized he had been spotted. Steele quickly stepped out from concealment and leveled his battle rifle at him.

"Move and you're dead."

"Don't shoot," the man said.

He was carrying a small two-way radio in his hand. He had it raised halfway up to his face and he had frozen in the act, afraid to move so much as a muscle.

"Go ahead," Steele said. "Make your call."

The man swallowed hard, not taking his eyes off Steele for a second. He raised the radio set up to his mouth and pressed the push-to-talk button.

"Come in, Gino."

"*Yeah, Shelly, go ahead.*"

"He hung a left on 57th, heading east. Over."

"*Got it. I'm right behind you. Stay loose. Don't let him spot you. Over.*"

"Right," said Shelly, his gaze riveted to Steele's.

Steele approached with his hand out. Moving very slowly, Shelly handed him the radio.

"How far back is he?" asked Steele.

"Three, maybe four blocks," Shelly said.

"On foot?"

"No, in a car."

"Who're you working for?"

The man hesitated.

"You've got about three seconds," Steele said, "then I'll kill you and ask your friend."

"Victor Borodini."

Steele's heart gave a leap. "God damn," he said, "it must be Christmas."

He stepped up to Shelly and quickly patted him down, relieving him of a 9mm., a .380, an eight-inch stiletto and two fragmentation grenades.

"Were these supposed to be for me?" Steele said, attaching the grenades to his belt. He tucked the 9mm. into his waistband at the small of his back and slipped the smaller .380 into his pocket. Shelly wisely chose not to reply.

"Sit down over here," said Steele, indicating a spot on the curb.

Apprehensively, Shelly did as he was told.

Steele took hold of an old, rusted parking meter that was stuck up out of the sidewalk at a crazy angle. He grabbed it with both hands, clamped down hard and pulled. Shelly watched with disbelief as the meter came loose from the sidewalk along with a hefty chunk of concrete. Steele bent down and wrapped the parking meter around him, trapping his arms. Shelly cried out with pain.

"Ahhh, *Jesus*! My *arms*! You're crushing them!"

"I'll crush a lot more than that if you don't shut the hell up," said Steele. "Now don't go 'way."

He left Shelly sitting on the curb with the meter wrapped around him and stepped back into the shadows. A moment later, a battered old Ford came cruising slowly around the corner. Gino spotted Shelly sitting on the curb and stopped the car.

"Shelly! What the fuck?"

He opened the car door and stepped out.

"Jesus fuckin' Christ," he said. "You let him spot you, didn't ya? You dumb shit, you're lucky he didn't—"

Steele stepped out of the shadows. "Hold it right there, Gino."

"Holy shit!"

Gino clawed for his shoulder holster and pulled out a .38 revolver. Steele raised his 4.3mm battle rifle with triple mode select-fire and 50-round capacity and said, "You've got to be kidding."

With an air of resignation, Gino dropped his gun.

"Open the back door," said Steele.

Gino complied.

"Now help your buddy in there," Steele said.

Gino helped Shelly to his feet. Stumbling under the weight of the parking meter with the attached lump of concrete, they made for the back door.

"This thing ain't gonna fit through," said Gino.

"Open the trunk," said Steele.

"Oh, Christ, no, not the trunk," moaned Shelly.

"Would you rather I just left you here?" asked Steele.

"No, no, that's okay," Shelly replied quickly. "The trunk'll be just fine."

Gino opened the trunk. Steele picked Shelly up as if he were a baby and dumped him in, meter and all. Shelly grunted with pain and the car rocked on its beat-up shocks, then Steele closed the trunk lid. Steele went around to the passenger side and opened the door.

"Get in, Gino. You're going to drive."

"Where to?"

"Where do you think, asshole? We're going to get my daughter."

The ringing phone woke Raven up. She sleepily reached across for Steele, but his side of the bed was empty. She sat up groggily and took a deep breath, rubbing her eyes. Steele hadn't been to bed. He must have gone out. Maybe Stalker had been sighted once again. The phone kept ringing. As she swung her legs over the side of the bed, she heard Jason answer it. She started to go out just as she was, then thought better of it and threw on a short silk robe. As she came out of the bedroom, she saw Jason standing with the phone up to his ear. His face was chalk white and he was trembling.

"What is it?" she said, suddenly wide awake.

"It's Stalker," Jason said. "And he's got Cory!"

Raven's eyes grew wide. She lunged for the speaker phone and switched it on.

"Who the hell *is* this?" she demanded. "Borodini, if that's you and—"

"Borodini's dead," said the coarse and hollow-sounding voice on the other end of the line. "And I've got the girl. Where's Steele?"

Raven felt her stomach knot up. "He . . . he's not here. I don't know where he is. Is Cory all right?"

"She's fine. And if her daddy wants to see her alive again, you tell him to come to me. Alone. We'll settle this just between the two of us. You tell Steele. Nobody else. I've cut out the trace that was on your line. If you call anyone else, I'll know and the girl will die. If Steele doesn't come alone, the girl will die. You tell him to go to Penn Station. Use the entrance off Seventh Avenue. I'll be waiting for him."

The line went dead.

"Oh, my God," said Raven.

"We've got to call Mr. Higgins!" Jason said.

"No," said Raven. "Stalker said if we called anyone else, he'd know and he'd kill Cory. He's tapped into the phone somehow."

"Jesus. So what do we *do*?" asked Jason, an agonized expression on his face.

Raven bit her lower lip and thought fast. "Run downstairs and get Ice—quickly."

Jason didn't even bother to dress. He bolted for the door in his bare feet and still wearing his father's bathrobe. Raven ran

back into the bedroom and started getting dressed. By the time
Jason got back with Ice, she was already dressed in jeans,
boots, a sweatshirt and a leather jacket over a bulletproof vest.
She had taken one of Steele's weapons harnesses and adjusted
it to fit her, then she holstered two Beretta 9mm.'s and slipped
several extra loaded magazines into the pouches. She was
sticking several hand grenades into her pockets when the door
opened and Jason came back in with Ice.

Though Jason had awakened him, the big man had dressed
quickly as soon as he heard what happened. "What the hell you
think you doin', girl?" he asked when he saw her.

"We've got to get to Higgins," she said. "He's the only one
who can reach Steele. They've got some kind of broadcast link
set up to reach him at the project lab."

"What's all the hardware for?" asked Ice.

"You don't think I'm gonna let Steele go in to face Stalker
all alone, do you? And I don't want any arguments, Ice. I've
been going crazy just sitting here and not knowing what the
hell was going on. I'm going and that's final."

She grabbed a machine pistol out of the arms cabinet,
slapped in a 50-round magazine of caseless ammo and grabbed
some spares.

"You crazy, girl," Ice said.

"I'm going to get dressed," said Jason. "I'm coming with
you."

"Jason, no! You're staying here."

"Forget about it!" Jason said. "She's *my* sister, God damn it!
and I know how to shoot a gun. Dad taught me. I'm a good
shot."

"Hey, boy, this ain't no target range we talkin' about," said
Ice.

"You're going to have to knock me out to stop me," Jason
said with grim determination. "I know you could, but when I
came to, I'd only follow you. I heard what Stalker said. I know
where he's holding Cory. What would you do if it was *your*
sister?"

Ice took a deep breath and let it out slowly. "Steele gonna
have my ass for this. All right, go throw some clothes on."

Jason rushed back into his room.

"You can't be serious," said Raven. "You're not really going to let him come?"

"What you want me to do, knock him on his ass?" said Ice, walking over to the arms cabinet and taking out a polymer/ceramic battle rifle.

"Yes, if you have to!" she said. "For God's sake, Ice, you'll only get him killed!"

"Shit, girl, we probably *all* gonna get killed. But I ain't much better at sittin' on my hands than you. And I ain't gonna ask the kid to do it. This be personal for him."

"Oh, Christ, don't hand me that macho shit! He's just a boy!"

"He be man enough. If we goin', he gotta right to come."

"Steele will never forgive you if anything happens to him."

"Yeah," said Ice. "Or you either. Want I should knock you out, too?"

She realized that further argument was useless. "At least make him wear a vest."

"Ain't gonna stop no plasma," Ice said.

"But at least it's *something*," she said. She went out on the balcony and looked toward the helipad. "Steele's chopper is still here. We can take it to the Federal Building. I'll go wake the pilot."

She ran out to the small guardhouse at the far end of the helipad.

Moments later, Jason was dressed and armed with a 9mm. semiauto, several grenades and a battle rifle. Ice checked the fit on his vest.

"You sure you know how to use them things?" he asked.

"I've never used grenades before," said Jason. "But you just pull the pin and throw, right?"

"Yeah, right," said Ice, shaking his head. "Come on."

They went out to the helipad. Raven was already standing by with the pilot, who had his VCASS helmet under his arm.

"Wait a minute," he said. "What's going on here? Where's Steele?"

"He ain't comin' on this trip," said Ice. "You gonna fly us over to the Federal Building."

"The hell I will," the pilot said. "I've got orders to stand by with this chopper for Lt. Steele. I'm not running any taxi service."

"Listen to me," Raven said, "Stalker's got Steele's daughter and he's threatening to kill her. Steele ain't here. We don't know where he is. We've got to get over to the Federal Building and let Higgins know, so he can get in touch with Steele on the broadcast link."

"Hell, why didn't you say so?" said the pilot. He hopped into the chopper and pulled on his helmet.

A couple of the roof guards came hurrying over.

"What's going on here?" one of them asked.

"We're taking the chopper over to the Federal Building," Raven said.

"I'm afraid I can't let you do that, ma'am," the guard said. "We've got strict orders from Lt. Steele not to let you folks leave the building."

"You don't understand," she said. "Stalker just called here. He's got Steele's daughter! We've got to get over to the Federal Building and see Higgins, so he can let Steele know!"

"You can call him from here, ma'am."

"I *can't* call him! Stalker's got the phone line tapped! He said he'd kill Cory if we called anyone! Steele's got to know!"

"You don't need all that ordnance just to deliver a message," said the guard. "The pilot can fly over to the Federal Building by himself and give Higgins the word. I don't know what you folks think you're doing, but you might as well forget it. We've got our orders. I'm sorry, but you're not going anywhere."

"Those orders apply to me, too, Tony?" said Ice, stepping up to the guard.

"No, we've got no orders about you, Ice. You can go. But Miss Scarpetti and the boy stay here."

Ice turned back to Raven and Jason. "Fraid we got no choice," he said. "You see how it is. You just gonna have to—"

Then he suddenly drove his elbow back hard into the guard's

solar plexus. The other two guards reacted immediately, bringing up their weapons. Ice managed to snatch the gun away from one of them, but the other one backed off and quickly worked the bolt on his rifle.

"Hold it right there, Ice!"

"Whatcha gonna do, Scott?" said Ice. "Shoot me?"

The chopper's engines started and the blades began to turn.

The man grimaced and lowered his weapon. "Damn it, Ice . . ."

"Go on," said Ice to Raven and Jason. "Get aboard."

"If I let you go, they're gonna have my ass for it," said Scott.

"Okay, I make it easy on you," Ice said. "When you wake up, tell Tony I was sorry I hadda hit him."

And he crashed a hard right into Scott's jaw.

The guard crumpled. Ice turned to the last guard.

"Joey . . ."

"Oh, what the hell," said Joey. "Go ahead."

Ice dropped him with one punch. Then he got into the chopper and it lifted off.

Higgins stood behind Jennifer Stone as she sat at the computer console in his office, staring with astonishment at the screen. Strings of alpha-numerical representations of data were flying by so fast that they were nothing but a blur.

"I'm getting no response whatsoever," she said, shaking her head. "There's nothing I can do to stop it."

They had already tried shutting the computer down. But it would not shut down. Jennifer had been working with the backup program when suddenly everything seemed to go haywire. The computer suddenly refused to respond to her keyboard commands. It was as if someone had taken it over. And then they realized that someone was accessing the computer through the modem. They had pulled the plug. And *still* the computer kept on working, flashing data across the screen at a dizzying rate.

"I don't believe it," Higgins said, staring at the screen with complete incomprehension. "How the hell can it keep on working with the plug pulled? Where's the damn *power* coming from?"

He ran over to the intercom on his desk. "Connors!" he shouted. "I want that goddamn trace! *Now*!"

"We're working on it, sir," the security chief's reply came over the speaker. "Should have it for you at any time now . . ."

"I don't want it anytime, I want it *now*, God damn it! Someone's accessing top secret project data through a restricted line! I want to know who it is and how the fuck they're doing it!"

"The phone line," Jennifer said, here eyes wide as she looked up from the screen.

"What?"

"The phone line! It's the only possible explanation. They're getting power to the computer through the phone line!"

"That's impossible. How the hell can they do that?"

"I don't know. But I can't think of any other explanation."

"Damn it!" Higgins said. "If I yank the line to the modem, we'll lose the fucking trace!"

"We've got it, Chief!" Connors voice came over the intercom. "Hang on a second, we'll have the name and address up in a second . . . What the hell?"

"What? What is it?" Higgins said.

"You're not gonna believe this, Chief. We've traced the call to Dr. Cooper's apartment."

"*Cooper*?" Higgins said. He frowned. "Are you absolutely sure?"

"No question, Chief. I'm sending a squad of men over right away to find out what the hell is going on over there."

"Dev Cooper's doing this?" asked Jennifer. "I can't believe it. He wouldn't have the skill to pull off something like this, unless he's been hiding it all along—"

"The *matrix*!" Higgins said, realization suddenly dawning. "Jesus Christ. It *has* to be! It's Cooper's copy of the program!"

He rushed over to the computer and ripped out the modem. The screen winked out.

Immediately, one of the screens in the wall console came on, flashing the same dizzying blur of data. Then another screen came on. And another one, and another one.

"*What the fuck is happening?*" said Higgins.

"It's transferred to the wall console through the power lines," said Jennifer with fascination. "They're interfacing. Cooper's copy of the matrix and ours are interfacing."

Higgins bent down over his intercom again. "Connors! When your people get to Cooper's place, have them shut down his computer *immediately*, do you understand? Pull the plug. Smash the motherfucking thing to pieces if you have to, but shut it down!"

"No!" said Jennifer, coming up behind him. "You can't!"

"The hell I can't! I'm cutting this off until I can find out what the hell is going on."

"If you cut it off now, we might never find out!" she said. "Something absolutely amazing is happening here, Oliver! Let it go! Let's see what happens!"

"No way," said Higgins with grim determination. "I've learned my lesson with Stalker. I'm not taking any chances. I'm stopping it right now until we can get some kind of handle on this."

He turned back to the intercom. "Connors, the minute your people get over there, I want an immediate report. I want to know what's going on there. I want—"

Jennifer suddenly grabbed his arm. "Oliver!"

The tone of her voice made him turn around immediately. He froze when he saw what was on the screens. The center screen in the wall console had ceased its blurring images of data and now showed something else entirely. One by one, the other screens stopped flashing data and switched to the same images as the ones in the central screen, until all of them were displaying the same thing.

A videotape of Higgins and Jennifer making love on the office desk.

"Oh, my God," said Higgins softly.

Jennifer was staring at the screens, speechless.

Higgins glanced up at the surveillance camera mounted under the ceiling in his office.

"You made a *tape* of us?" said Jennifer, turning to him with shocked disbelief.

"No, of course not," Higgins said, still staring at the camera. "That camera was off. I only have it switched on when I leave the office. The goddamn matrix must have switched it on somehow. The bastard made a tape of us!"

"Is anyone *else* seeing this?" she asked in a shocked voice, her gaze riveted to the images of herself and Higgins coupling passionately on the desk.

"No," said Higgins. "At least, I don't think so. How could they? Unless . . ."

He spun around and hit the button on the intercom. "Connors!"

"They should be getting there any minute, Chief—"

"Never mind that! I want all power to this office shut down *now*! Right *now* right this *instant*!"

There was a brief silence.

"Connors? Do you *hear* me?"

"I . . . I'm not sure I know how to do that, sir. I'll have to get the building engineers—"

"*Do it!* Whatever it takes, *do it!* But do it *now*! I want all the power in here *off*!"

"Oliver . . ." she said, clutching his arm. "I'm scared."

"Take it easy," he said. "We're going to get this under control."

But he didn't sound so sure.

Then, suddenly, one by one, the screens winked off.

But the office lights stayed on. The power hadn't been cut off yet.

"What happened?" Higgins said.

Jennifer slowly shook her head. "I don't know."

They stood there and stared at the dark screens for what seemed like a long time, and then suddenly the lights in the office went out.

"They've cut the power," Higgins said. He took Jennifer by the arm. "Come on."

They left the office and hurried down the hall to the office of the Chief of Project Security.

"What's going on?" asked Higgins as they went in.

Connors was seated at his desk, wearing a headset. "The power off?" he asked.

"Yeah, it just went off. What's happening?"

Connors held up a finger. He was listening. "They just got to Cooper's place," he said. "They had to break in. Cooper's passed out on his couch, dead drunk."

"What about his computer?" Jennifer asked.

Connors relayed the question into the tiny headset mike. "It was on when they came in," he said. "But they say there's nothing on the screen. It's blank. There's nothing booted up."

"That can't be," said Higgins. "There's got to be software in the drives. Have them check it out."

Connors passed the order on. They waited tensely.

Connors looked up at them.

"They say it's blank," he said.

"What do you mean, it's blank?" said Higgins.

"Erased," Connors replied. "Wipe clean. Cooper's out like a light and there was no one else in the apartment.

Higgins frowned. "It doesn't make any sense."

"What do you want to do about Cooper?" Connors asked.

"Have him brought here. I don't care if they have to carry him, but I want him back here on the double."

Connors relayed the order. A buzzer went off and a light on his desk console came on. He stabbed a button.

"Connors," he said. "This better be important. We've got a situation here . . ."

They could hear the caller through the console speaker.

"It's Sgt. Flaherty, sir, down at the lab. There's something funny going on down here. Some of the workers finishing up here said a bunch of the data banks came on all of a sudden, by themselves. They swear they haven't touched anything, but somebody must have tripped a switch or something, I don't know. I tried calling Dr. Stone at her office, but there's no answer—"

Jennifer turned and bolted from the office.

"Stand by, Flaherty, she's on her way down," said Connors. He looked up at Higgins, "What the hell is going on?"

But Higgins was already running out the door.

Cory was more frightened and confused than ever. They had taken the freight elevator down to the basement level, and just before the doors opened, Stalker had shoved her into a corner at the front of the elevator, telling her to crouch down and not move. Then he inserted fresh magazines into his AK-47s and stood in front of the door, holding one in each hand by the wood pistol grips. The doors slid open, but nothing happened. Stalker turned to Cory and told her to follow him.

She got up quickly and went out into the basement . . . and froze, her eyes and mouth opened wide in horror. The walls of the basement were pockmarked with bulletholes and the floor was littered with bodies and sticky with blood. The large, heavy steel-reinforced door to the passageway leading to the subway tunnel had been smashed in and it lay on the floor. Two legs were sticking out from beneath it.

"Come on!" said Stalker. "Hurry up!"

As he spoke, she heard the sound of footsteps running down the stairs.

Stalker grabbed her roughly by the arm and shoved her toward the passageway. As he turned, several of Borodini's soldiers came running down the stairs into the basement. They opened up on him with assault rifles and Viper machine pistols. Cory stared with shocked disbelief as the bullets slammed into his chest. He staggered backward from the impact, but he didn't fall. Ragged holes appeared in his jumpsuit. One bullet tore off a piece of his right ear. Another creased his scalp. His head snapped back sharply as another struck him in the forehead, just above his left eye, and ricocheted off his nysteel skull casing. But he didn't even seem to feel it.

He opened up with both assault rifles, sweeping the stairs leading down to the basement. Men screamed and their bodies tumbled down to the foot of the stairs, piling up into bloody, bullet-shredded heaps. Stalker turned, blood streaming from his ear, but there was no blood coming from the wounds in his scalp and forehead. No blood coming from the bullet holes in his chest and upper thighs. The polymer skin on his scalp and forehead was torn from the impact of the bullets and gleaming nysteel showed through. His eyes were glowing red fire.

Cory cried out and shrank from him in fear. He threw down one of the empty rifles and grabbed her by the hand, pulling her down the passageway after him. She had to run to keep up. Several times she stumbled, but he didn't stop. He just kept pulling her on. They reached the end of the passageway and came out into a dark subway tunnel. There were no lights in the tunnel, but Stalker's eyes suddenly flared with a bright, white-yellow light and twin beams shot out from his eyes, illuminating the tunnel in front of them. He pushed her ahead of him.

"Come on," he said. "Move! Quickly!"

Dazed, she went in front of him, her form silhouetted in bright beams coming from his eyes. Her mind was numb with overload. They moved through the tunnels for what seemed like an impossibly long time, turning from one tunnel into another until she had lost all sense of where they were or what direction they were heading in. She wept and cried out in revulsion as rats skittered across her feet. They moved down the dank, musty tunnels and she kept tripping on the tracks, stumbling over piles of refuse that smelled terrible. She did not look down. She was afraid to see what they were.

They came upon a hideously decomposing body of some tunnel dweller, or perhaps one of their victims, slumped against the tunnel wall, the flesh shriveled with the bones showing through, the teeth horribly exposed in a death rictus. Rats crawled over the corpse and maggots writhed in what was left of the torso. Cory started screaming. She couldn't stop. Her screams echoed through the tunnel like the whistle of a train.

Stalker pulled on her arm and she was yanked off balance. She fell against him, but she still couldn't stop screaming. Then it all became too much for her conscious mind to bear. Her eyes rolled up and she fainted.

Effortlessly, Stalker lifted her up and slung her over his

shoulder. He turned off his illuminating beams. He didn't need them now. He could see perfectly in the dark, and he didn't need to worry about the girl tripping over things she couldn't see. He continued walking through the tunnels. Soon, he could see the light of a campfire in the distance. They were close to Pennsylvania Station.

He left the unconscious girl with the tunnel dwellers, giving them strict orders not to touch her. A few of them stared at her with either sexual or physical hunger, perhaps both, but he didn't need to worry about their disobedience. He told them that if he returned and found her harmed in any way, he would kill all of them.

He went to make the call to Steele. When Jason answered the phone, a flicker of recognition passed through him at the sound of the boy's voice, but he forced it away. He didn't want to be distracted. It was becoming increasingly difficult for him to concentrate. He was experiencing violent mood swings. One moment, he would feel elated, as he had when they had hit the Dragons. That, he felt, had been a good thing, though he wasn't certain why, but it had made him feel good. For a while, the fever in his cybernetic brain abated. But after he had tapped into the line and made the call, he was once more plunged deep into black depression.

He remained monitoring the phone network for a while, his brain keyed to remain alert for any call emanating from Steele's number, but meanwhile, he simply scanned the network, listening in to different conversations, different slices of the human condition unfolding in the city above him.

One man was calling home to his family, telling his wife that he would be forced to work late at the office and he'd be late for dinner. His wife sounded disappointed. The children were back with their grandparents and she had prepared a special dinner for him. The same thing they'd had when they first met. It was their tenth anniversary and she had planned a special evening for them.

"*I've even put on the same dress I was wearing when we had our first date,*" she said.

"*Really? You mean that slinky blue one?*"

"Yes. I got it out of storage. Would you believe that it still fits me?"

"Yeah, I'd believe it," he said.

"I've got the table all set and I've got the candles out . . ."

"Oh, honey . . ."

"Well . . . that's okay. Dinner will keep, I guess." She sighed with resignation. *"Will you be very late?"*

"I'll try to wind things up here as quickly as I can, I promise."

"You do what you have to do," she said. *"I'll wait."*

"I love you."

"I love you, too."

He monitored another call.

" . . . thinking about you all day."

"Were you really?"

"I can't seem to get you out of my mind."

"I've been thinking about you, too."

"When can I see you again?"

"Tomorrow night?"

"How about dinner? I know a nice little Italian place over on 86th. Great food, dim lights, soft music . . ."

"You like Italian food?"

"I love it. Why, don't you?"

"Are you kidding? I'm half Italian. I've got a better idea. Why don't I make dinner for you?"

"You're kidding. You can cook, too?"

"I make a lasagna you would die for. And we could dim the lights and put on some music . . ."

"Sounds very romantic. What time do you want me there?"

"Sevenish? That'll give me time to take a bath and put on something comfortable."

"You want your back scrubbed?"

"No, I think I can manage. Besides, if we start with that, we might never get to dinner. And I want to show off my cooking."

"I'll be there at seven on the dot."

"Okay, then. Oh, and one more thing . . ."

"What's that?"

"Bring your toothbrush."

As he scanned the network and listened in on idle bits of conversation, Stalker grew more and more depressed. These people had lives. They lived, they loved, they fought, they struggled, they survived. And what did he have? He had nothing. Nothing but fleeting glimpses of past lives that were his, and yet not his. Nothing but a maelstrom of emotions that pulled him in different directions at once. Nothing but self-loathing for what he was and a surging hatred for those who'd made him that way.

He recalled hearing the voice of Dr. Phillip Gates as he was brought on line. A voice filled with pride and excitement.

"He should be waking up any second now. God, I'm as nervous as a schoolboy getting ready for his first date. Stalker's going to bowl them over. My greatest achievement! When they see what he can do, they'll be falling all over themselves to fund the Steele Project!"

And then the voice faded away and he heard another one, the voice of a small girl, laughing as he bounced her on his knee, the twin boys laughing, too, and shouting, *"Me next, Daddy! Me next!"* And he saw his wife beaming at them as they played in the living room . . . but he didn't know the woman and he had no idea who the children were. Voices, voices, voices . . . memories with nothing to be rooted in, a cornucopia of confusing and conflicting images, whirling through his mind like a howling hurricane.

He disengaged from the network and grabbed his head, doubling over and groaning. He smashed his fist into the wall, again and again and again, and yet again, but it didn't help. There was no pain to drive away the fever in his computer brain; the wall merely crumbled into dust and fragments of broken concrete. He screamed with rage, agony and frustration, and the sound echoed through the darkness.

He tried with every ounce of will he had to focus in on just one thing. *Steele.* It was Steele who was responsible. It was because of Steele that they did this to him. It was the Steele Project that had brought him all this torment. And it was Steele who would pay. Slowly, the jumble of confusing images and voices faded, to be replaced by a grim purpose, the resolution of a mission that had to be accomplished, the programmed imperative taking over, the mission, the mission, accomplish the mission, let nothing interfere, destroy the enemy . . .

And that enemy was Steele.

10

The technicians and workers stood around the lab, confused and puzzled, frightened of the soldiers standing there with their weapons and refusing to allow anyone to leave, mystified as to what was happening around them. All the machines were running. They had simply come on all by themselves. Data flickered across the screens at an impossible rate of speed. Every data bank within the lab was being accessed. And none of them knew how.

Jennifer Stone rushed around the lab, trying to shut down the computers, but she was having no more luck than she had up in Higgins' office. She ran from keyboard to keyboard, but she could get no response to her commands. She flicked the power switches, all to no avail.

"Rip out the power lines!" said Higgins. "All of them!"

"I can't," she said. "They're all hardwired. We'd have to rip up the floor and tear out all the cables. . . ."

"Well, do something, for God's sake! Shut down all power to the lab!"

"If we did that now, we could lose irreplaceable data," she said.

"Damn it!" Higgins swore.

The soldiers stood around nervously, knowing that something was terribly wrong, but not knowing what it was and not knowing what, if anything, they were supposed to do about it.

"It's here," said Higgins. "It came down through the goddamn power lines! It's raiding all our data!"

"Not it," said Jennifer. "*He*. And I don't see what we can do about it. We'll simply have to let it run its course and see what happens."

"Damn it, I need Cooper down here!" Higgins said. "He's been talking with this thing. Maybe he can stop it. Maybe he can tell us what the hell it wants."

"Not *it*," said Jennifer again. "That's Steele in there. His electronic twin. And if you ask me, he wants everything. Dev Cooper couldn't give him the right answers. So he came to get them for himself."

"What the hell are we supposed to do?" asked Higgins.

Jennifer shook her head. "I don't know," she said. "All we can do is wait and see."

One of the soldiers came hurrying up to them. "Sir, there's a call for you from the security station up on the roof."

"Christ, what *now*?" said Higgins. He hurried to a phone and picked it up. "Higgins," he said.

"Sir, Steele's chopper just landed on the helipad, but Steele's not aboard. It's three civilians. They say their names are Ice, Raven Scarpetti and Jason Steele, the lieutenant's son. And they're demanding to speak with you at once. They say it's an extreme emergency."

"All right, put Ice on."

A moment later, Ice's unmistakable deep rumbling voice came over the phone.

"That you, Higgins?"

"What's going on, Ice? Why are you here? Where's Steele?"

"Don't know," said Ice. "We got us a problem. Steele took off somewhere. Took his full battle kit. And Stalker just called. Said he got Steele's daughter. Wants Steele to meet him at Penn Station. Said to come alone or else he'd kill the girl. We couldn't call 'cause Stalker done tapped into the phone somehow. You gotta get Steele on that broadcast link and let him know."

"I'll get right on it," Higgins said. "You three better come on down. Tell security to take you to my office . . . no, wait.

Better not. Have them take you down to Dr. Stone's office. I'll meet you there in just a—"

"No can do, Mr. H. We gonna take us a little trip out to Pennsylvania Station."

"Are you crazy? Stay the hell away from there! I want you to—"

The line went dead.

Ice had ripped the phone wire out of the receiver. He held it up to show the guard and shrugged. "Shit, look what I went and done. Must be nerves, man. Sorry 'bout the phone. We leavin' now."

He hurried back out to the chopper pad as the guard stared after him, perplexed.

Down in the lab, Higgins suddenly realized that he didn't know if he could get Steele on the broadcast link. Not with that . . . that *thing*, no matter what Jennifer said it was, apparently in control of the lab. But at least the phones were still working. He dialed Connors' extension.

"Connors."

"It's Higgins, Andy. Stalker's at Penn Station. Alert the task force. And tell them to be careful. He might have Steele's daughter with him. Get out the call, I'll get right back to you."

"Right. I'm on it."

Higgins hung up the phone. Jennifer was staring at him. She had overheard what he said.

"I need that broadcast link for Steele," he said. "Can we get through to him?"

"I don't know," she said. "I've never used it before. I've read the files on it, but that's not the same as—"

Suddenly, all the machines started to shut down.

Jennifer moistened her lips. "You don't think he heard us?" she said.

"I don't know," said Higgins. "The lab's wired for sound, as part of the security system. It's possible that—"

Jennifer didn't wait to listen to the rest of it. She ran over to one of the consoles and punched in a code.

"It's responding now," she said.

HIggins came up behind her.

She started to call up the sequence for the broadcast link to Steele's cybernetic brain, but the program came up at once, before she could even finish.

"Jesus, this is scary," she said.

She typed in the commands to activate the signal.

They waited.

"Okay," she said, after a moment, taking a deep breath. "I'm getting through."

She started typing out the message.

Steele held the tunnel dweller up against the wall by his throat. The filthy, scrofulous man stared at him, eyes wide with terror. His companions lay on the tracks around them, some unconscious, some dead, some moaning from their injuries. They had heard him coming down the tunnel and had hidden in the service niches, waiting for him to get closer, but it had not turned out at all the way they'd planned.

They'd jumped him when he got close, but he was ready for them. Too late, they saw that he was armed, but he didn't even shoot. He simply clubbed them down with the rifle, tore them from his back with one hand and flung them with incredible force against the tunnel walls, knocked them down and crushed their skulls with just one blow, moving so quickly and fighting back with such incredible strength that it was over in a matter of seconds. Now the one remaining derelict gazed with fear into those horrible, red-glowing eyes, not even trying to struggle against the powerful grip that held him.

"Where's Stalker?" Steele said. "Another one just like me, he's hiding down here somewhere with you scum. *Where is he?*"

The terrified derelict shook his head and made small whimpering noises.

"*Talk*, you miserable son of a—"

Suddenly, Steele stiffened.

A message was coming through the broadcast link.

As he received it, a chill went through him.

He took the tunnel dweller and tossed him aside as if he were a doll then ran full speed down the tracks.

• • •

The chopper set down at Pennsylvania Plaza, near the corner of West 33rd and Eighth. The pilot turned back toward them, his voice sounding tinny through the speaker of his VCASS helmet.

"The task force's moving in," he said. "I'm monitoring their communications. All units are converging on Penn Station."

"We better get a move on, then," said Ice. "They get here before we go down, they probably try to stop us."

"I should probably try to stop you, too," the pilot said.

"Yo, Jason, watch what the hell you doin', boy," Ice said. "That grenade done gonna fall outta your right pocket!"

"What?" said Jason, looking down.

Ice crashed his fist into his jaw. The boy crumpled in the seat.

"Take 'im back," Ice said to the pilot. "And *sit* on 'im."

"You got it," said the pilot. "Watch yourselves down there. I'll radio the task force that you're goin' down, so they don't shoot you by mistake."

"'Preciate that," said Ice.

"They're not gonna be happy about it, but I'll tell 'em you held a gun to my head. Good luck."

They got out and he lifted off, heading back toward the penthouse.

They ran toward the entrance to the station. It had once been the main railroad terminal in New York City, connecting with subway lines running uptown and downtown and trains heading out to Long Island, with an Amtrak Terminal that had lines running to Providence and Boston and points north, to Philadelphia and Washington, D. C. and points south and west across the country. It was a huge complex underneath Madison Square Garden, and it had once held rows of shops and restaurants, bars and newsstands and even an Off-Track Betting parlor.

Now it was deserted, a shelter for only the most desperate of homeless derelicts. The stairs and floors were littered with trash and soiled with human excrement. The ticket counters had been broken up for fuel and the shops were empty, the windows smashed, the interiors gutted, many of them burned. The railroad lines no longer ran; the only way out of the city was by road across the bridges in protected convoys.

There was no power down here anymore. The only illumination came from the fires burning in metal garbage cans, dimly lighting up the ruined booths and storefronts that had once sold books and men's apparel, chocolates and newspapers, magazines, beer, hot dogs, fresh clams brought in from the Long Island shore. A haze of smoke hung in the air from the cans out in the corridors and fires built inside the storefronts, where shadowy figures huddled together for warmth and stared out at them with glittering eyes.

It was like entering another world. And somewhere, in this huge charnelhouse of human refuse, Stalker was hiding with Cory Steele. Hiding . . . and waiting.

"You think he really got the girl?" Ice said as they moved cautiously forward.

"I believed him," Raven said. "He said he killed Borodini. He must've traced him down somehow."

"Poor kid been through the mill, all right," said Ice. "Think she still alive?"

"It would make sense for him to use her as a hostage," Raven said. "But we can't let Stalker call the shots. He's insane. There's no guarantee that he'll let Cory live, no matter what we do. And Steele knows that, too. I just hope he gets here in time."

"Don't think about it," Ice said. "Just watch yourself. There be a lot of crazies down here."

Even as he spoke, several groups of men and women, bedraggled and disheveled, came shambling out of several dark storefronts up ahead to either side of them. More came from a corridor leading off to the side. Raven quickly glanced around and saw that there was more behind them, cutting them off.

The shambling, tattered figures started moving toward them.

Ice turned on the laser sighting system on his battle rifle and a thin, bright red beam of light stabbed out toward them. Raven did the same. They scattered, scuttling back into the shadows. They knew what laser sighting systems were. They'd seen them before when Strike Force squads came down into the station periodically to clean them out, never with complete success.

Raven exhaled heavily. "Maybe we bit off a bit more than we could chew," she said nervously.

Ice chuckled. "Count on it," he said. He switched off the laser sighting system. "Better move soft and move slow. Some of 'em might not scare so easy."

They took the stairs down to the section of the station where the terminal for the Long Island Railroad had once been located. More fires burned down here in rusted and blackened metal cans, but there was no sign of any derelicts. Ice hesitated at the foot of the stairs, listening.

"Don't wanna sound like no cliché," he said, "but it just too damn quiet down here."

Off to their right, set back from the lobby of the terminal, was a seating area. Most of the chairs had long since been ripped out. They could see ragged blankets and soiled rags, old newspapers and mattresses scattered around the floor, but no one bedding down. Nor could they see all the way back into the shadows.

To their left were several sliding metal doors that opened to the stairs leading down to the tracks. The doors were open and there was nothing but darkness beyond. Farther up ahead, in the center of the lobby, were the remains of an information booth that had been busted down for firewood. Beyond that were old, abandoned storefronts running up and down the length of the lobby, shattered glass from their windows covering the floor, impenetrable darkness within. The concourse opened out into a T shape at that point, with Raven and Ice standing at the bottom. Ahead and to their left was a wide concourse going past abandoned, ruined storefronts, leading to the old downtown subway lines. To the right, the concourse ran past the old ticket counter, which had been torn down at some point, and narrowed at the end near the remains of a refreshment stand and a bar, where it became a corridor leading to the uptown lines and stairs to the street level. A lot of space. A lot of darkness, dimly illuminated by flickering flames and heavily shadowed.

"I don't like it any better than you do," Raven said. "Why didn't any of them come down here?"

She looked behind her.

Dark figures stood clustered at the top of the stairs, but they made no move to come down after them.

"He's down here somewhere," Raven said tensely. "I just know it. I hope like hell Higgins got through to Steele. I'd hate the thought of just the two of us down here alone."

"Bit too late to be thinkin' 'bout that," said Ice wryly. "'Sides, the task force bound to be gettin' down any time. Stalker done boxed hisself in."

"Maybe that's exactly what he wants," said Raven.

It was very quiet.

Suddenly, they heard the telltale click of a bolt being drawn back.

Ice spun toward the sound and fired.

The staccato rattle of the battle rifle echoed loudly through the concourse. They heard the sound of a body falling and the clatter of a weapon on the floor. Immediately, other weapons opened up, assault rifles, semiautomatics and machine pistols. Ice grabbed Raven and pulled her down to the floor. Bullets thudded into the walls around them and went whining off the stairs.

And then they heard a voice shouting over the crashing of the guns.

"Cease fire! Cease fire!"

"C'mon!" Ice said. "Crawl on your belly!"

They wriggled toward the waiting area to their right, where they could take shelter behind a pile of rubble and the wall.

"Steele!" a hoarse, metallic-sounding voice called out. *"Steele!"*

"I think we found him," Raven said.

"More like he found us," said Ice. "I didn't bargain on him havin' no army. We in a pack of trouble."

"Where the hell *are* they?" Raven said.

"Up ahead, in the main concourse, hiding out inside the stores," said Ice.

"Steele! Come on out, Steele! I've got your daughter! Come on out and meet me!"

"We need us some more light down here," said Ice.

He reached into his pocket and pulled out an incendiary grenade. He yanked the pin and counted, then got up to his knees and lobbed it toward the wreckage of the information booth in the center of the concourse. The grenade hit and went off with a concussive roar and a huge wash of flame, lighting up the entire concourse around it, illuminating shabby figures with automatic weapons standing in the storefront entrances and crouching in the shattered window displays. Ice and Raven opened fire, sweeping their laser sights across the row of ruined stores. The tunnel dwellers jerked and fell. Some of them took off running, away from the line of fire. Ice and Raven cut them down as they ran, but others got away, down both ends of the concourse, while others still retreated back into the darkness of the stores and returned their fire.

For what seemed like a long time, the crackle of automatic weapons fire echoed through the concourse, then they heard Stalker screaming for them to cease fire once again. The weapons fire gradually died away.

Ice and Raven heard the sound of running footsteps and gunfire from the corridors above them.

"Damn you, Steele! I said to come alone! Your daughter's gonna die for this!"

"Steele ain't here!" shouted Ice.

"What're you doing?" Raven said.

"Playin' for time," Ice said.

"Who are you? Where's Steele?"

Raven heard sounds behind them and to their left. She turned and saw black clad figures in full riot gear crawling down the old rusted and frozen escalator, using its waist-high metal walls to shield them from fire.

"Over here!" she hissed.

"Raven? That you?"

She didn't recognize the voice, but a moment later, a man

wearing full riot gear complete with computer backpack equipped with rocket launchers and battle helmet came crawling into the darkened waiting area, his assault rifle cradled in his elbows. He was followed by several of his men. In their black fatigues, they blended with the shadows and moved down into the lower terminal like ghosts. She couldn't see his face behind the shield, though with the image intensifier and infra-red systems built into his helmet, he could see clearly in the darkness.

"Lt. Volkirk," he said.

"Am I glad to see you," Raven said with relief.

"Are you two out of your fuckin' minds?" said Volkirk. "Get the hell outta here! We'll cover you. We've got the entire place surrounded, units comin' down from all sides. This place is gonna get damned hot in about 30 seconds!"

"It's already damned hot," Raven said. "And we're not going anywhere. If your people start shooting at anything that moves, you're liable to hit Cory. She's down here with Stalker somewhere."

"There's nothing I can do about that," Volkirk said grimly. "We've got our orders. Stalker doesn't get out of here alive. We can't take any chances. We'll blow the whole damn place up if we have to."

"And what about Cory?" asked Raven.

"She's expendable," said Volkirk.

"She's *what*?" asked Raven with disbelief.

"Look, I don't like it any better than you do," Volkirk said heavily. "I'm sorry, but I've got my orders."

"You just got new orders," Raven said, levelling her rifle at him.

Several of Volkirk's men immediately brought their weapons up, but he quickly held up his hand, holding them off.

"Don't be stupid," he said. "You can shoot me, but that won't change a thing. My people will still carry out their orders."

"*Steele*!" Stalker called out again from somewhere in the concourse. "*I want Steele! Steele, where the hell are you?*"

"I'm right here, Mick," they suddenly heard Steele call out. "Everybody hold your fire!"

"Hot damn," said Ice.

"Thank God," Raven said. "Where is he?"

Volkirk shook his head. "I don't know. I can't see him. Can't tell where the hell anybody is with all the echo down here." He spoke into his helmet mike. "This is Volkirk. Everybody hold their positions. Hold your fire unless attacked. Repeat, hold your fire unless attacked."

"I'm the one you want, Mick," Steele called out. "Send Cory out. We'll settle this just between ourselves. That's what you wanted, isn't it, Mick?"

"Don't call me that!"

"Why not? It's your name, Mick, remember? You're Mick Taylor. We used to be partners, Mick. We used to be friends."

"Shut up! Shut up!"

"I loved you like a brother, Mick. Cory loved you. She used to call you Uncle Mick, remember? You used to bounce her on your knee when she was just a baby. You don't really want to hurt her, do you, Mick?"

"Damn you! I said to come alone! It's all your fault! I said to come alone or else I'd kill her!"

"If it was up to me, Mick, I would've come alone, believe me. But it wasn't up to me. I didn't bring those people, you did."

"You're trying to confuse me!"

"You *are* confused, Mick. You're confused and you're hurting. I know. Let me try to help you."

"Help me? Like you helped me before? You left me to die, you bastard!"

"That isn't true, Mick," Steele called out. They still could not see where either of them were. "I didn't leave you. I was hit, too."

"You're lying! You got me killed! But they wouldn't let me stay dead! They brought me back! Made me into some goddamn machine!"

"I know, Mick. Believe me, I know. They did it to me, too. But you can live with this, you really can. There's something wrong with your mind. You're sick. Come back with me, Mick. Please. Let me help you. They can fix it."

"No! I don't want to be like this!" His voice was a hysterical half-scream, half-sob. *"Why couldn't they let me die? Why did you have to make them do this? Why? I'm gonna kill you for letting them do this to me! I'm gonna kill you, you lousy son of a bitch! You're gonna pay! You're all gonna pay!"*

"Okay, Mick. If that's the way you want it. But let Cory go. Please. She never did anything to you. She's been hurt enough. She loved you, Mick. Let her go and I'll do anything you want. I'll send everyone away and it'll be just you and me. I promise. Send her out."

Silence.

They all waited tensely.

Then they heard a frightened young girl's voice call out, "Daddy?"

"Units 3 and 4, start moving in," Volkirk said into his helmet mike.

"What the hell you *doin'*, man?" said Ice.

"I can't take any chances," Volkirk said. "I need to make sure all exits from the concourse are covered."

"Stop it!" Raven said. "Send them back! Wait till she's clear!"

"Daddy, where are you?"

"I'm over here, honey. I can see you. Come on, keep coming straight ahead."

"God damn it, Volkirk, tell them to pull back!" said Raven.

They could now see Cory illuminated by the flames as she moved out into the center of the concourse. And then someone yelled out a warning and opened fire.

All hell broke loose.

Several other weapons opened up from the ruined storefronts and Volkirk's men started to return the fire.

"Daddeeeee!"

Cory screamed and fell.

"NO!"

"Oh, Jesus . . ." Raven said.

"Move in!" Volkirk shouted into his helmet mike. "All units, move in *now*!"

Several rockets were launched and they struck the storefronts where the fire was coming from. Flames and smoke belched forth as the rockets exploded, men screamed, debris flew. . . .

The task force units started moving in, firing as they went. Raven saw Steele running out into the center of the concourse, heedless of the hail of bullets, bending over Cory, and then Raven was running herself, ignoring Ice crying out for her to stop. She kept on running and suddenly she was tackled from behind. She went down hard.

Ice threw himself on top of her.

"Let me go! God damn you, let me *go*!"

Steele had Cory in his arms and he was running toward them, bent over, trying to shield his daughter with his body. Volkirk and his men went running past them.

"Steele!" cried Raven. "Over here!"

Ice got up as he came running toward them.

"Get her out of here," said Steele. "Get her to a hospital!"

Ice took Cory from his arms and started sprinting back toward the stairs.

"Go with him," Steele said to Raven. "Help her, *please*."

They heard a *whump* as a blast of plasma struck Volkirk and his advancing unit. The men screamed as they were incinerated.

"*Go!*" said Steele.

For a moment, but only just a moment, Raven hesitated, then turned and ran after Ice. In that moment, she had seen the blood on Steele's face where the bullets had struck him, ripping through the soft human flesh of his cheek and taking away most of his left ear. His clothes were riddled with bullet holes and the polymer flesh was torn away from his scalp, hanging in flaps along with his synthetic hair, exposing the bright nysteel skull casing beneath. As she turned and ran after Ice, tears streamed down her cheeks.

Steele turned and ran back into the heat of battle. More plasma bursts were fired, one right after the other, and police and derelicts alike went up in flames, many of them burned to a crisp before they knew what hit them, others turned into human torches as they ran, screaming in agony and wreathed in fire. The remaining tunnel dwellers had enough. Many of them threw down their weapons and ran panic-stricken for the nearest exits or for the subway tunnels. But wherever they ran, they encountered Strike Force units and were cut down by a withering hail of fire.

Steele released the lock on his left hand and twisted if off at the wrist, snapping it onto one of the special locking discs on his weapons belt. Then he stuck his stump of a wrist into the machine pistol attachment on his belt, felt it click into place and snapped it free. The machine pistol was now a part of him, fully thought-controlled, slaved to his cybernetic brain. Holding the battle rifle by its pistol grip in his right hand, he ran in the direction that the plasma bursts had come from, his eyes glowing red as his laser designator system switched in.

Stalker had fled down the far end of the concourse, firing plasma as he ran, burning down Strike Force units that tried to block his way. One officer managed to throw a grenade before he died; it went off in the cyborg's path, peppering him with shrapnel. He felt no pain. He simply kept on moving, mowing down anyone in his way.

He reached one of the subway platforms and ploughed through the iron gate, tearing it off its hinges. He jumped down onto the tracks and started running down the tunnel.

He knew that Steele would follow him. He was counting on it. It was what he wanted.

The two of them alone.

Steele leaped over the burning bodies and ran out onto the subway platform. Behind him, the sounds of the battle were starting to die down. Most of it was over. But for him, the final battle was only just beginning. He had the image of his daughter's torn and bleeding body in his mind and cold rage surged through him like a cataract.

He stopped and listened. His left ear was no longer functional, but he could still hear out of his right. He turned it up full and heard the sound of running footsteps in the distance, down the tunnel to his right. He leaped down onto the tracks and gave pursuit.

He ran at full speed down the dark tunnel, but he knew that he would not catch Stalker until he was ready to turn and fight. Judging the distance by the sound of Stalker's running footsteps, he could tell that the renegade cyborg was faster then he was. He refused to think of it as Mick. It wasn't Mick. Mick Taylor was dead. This was a killer machine.

And he was going to dismantle it.

Smash it into a thousand pieces.

Or die in the attempt.

They were underneath Times Square now, following the old, abandoned IRT Broadway-7th Avenue line, heading uptown. Stalker kept on moving ahead of him. Steele ran with everything he had, but he couldn't close the distance between them. Past 50th Street, heading toward Columbus Circle. They were heading toward the heart of Midtown.

Suddenly the tunnel ahead of him glowed with intense light and Steele ducked back into a service niche just in time as the plasma blast hurtled past him, searing him with its heat. He felt the human flesh on his face blister, crackle and peel, the polymer skin over his scalp and forehead start to melt. His hair caught fire. He paid no attention to it, letting it burn and switching off the pain circuits in his brain as he took off down the tunnel once again, firing his battle rifle as he ran.

At Columbus Circle, Stalker left the tracks and jumped up onto the platform. Steele swore under his breath as he realized that he was heading up into the streets. He jumped up onto the platform and ran for the stairs, taking them three and four at a time until he reached the street.

It was deserted.

He stopped and listened, sweeping the area with his optical systems on image intensifier and maximum zoom.

There.

Stalker was heading into Central Park.

They skirted the old Hecksher Playground, heading in a northeasterly direction, past the pond and towards Wollman

Rink. And it was there that Stalker stopped, in the old rink, standing in the center of it, waiting for him.

They stood facing each other like two wounded gladiators, part bleeding flesh, part damaged machine. The red lights glowing in Stalker's eyes allowed for no human expression. The chunks of flesh torn away by bullets revealed cold, unfeeling nysteel. He stood there, a creature born of nature and technology run wild, the thing that was once Mick Taylor, but that had now become a mockery of a human being, a mockery just as Steele himself was, the hair and synthetic skin burned from his head, his features a horrible mass of melted polymer and blackened flesh, his soul tormented, encased in circuitry, electrical synapses crackling with rage. Blood and bone and steel, crying out for human revenge. Steel justice.

"Neither of us has any business being alive," said Stalker, his voice a horrible metallic snarl. "Come on! Let's finish it!"

Steele raised his battle rifle and machine pistol and opened up with both on full auto.

Stalker jerked and staggered backward as the bullets struck him in the chest, shredding his clothes, but he did not go down. Steele kept up the stream of fire until both weapons were empty, but still the cyborg stood. He raised his arm and Steele leaped to one side as the plasma charge whooshed past him, striking the trees behind him and setting them aflame. Steele hit the ground and rolled, dropping his empty rifle as he came up and pulling out a magazine filled with high-explosive rounds. Stalker fired another blast of plasma, and Steele leaped again, diving and rolling out of the way as the blast ploughed into the ground. Stalker fired again. The firing mechanism cycled, but no blast of searing plasma came forth. He tried again with no result. He had run out of charges.

Steele slapped the magazine into his pistol attachment and brought it up, aiming at Stalker's head, but the other cyborg was too fast for him. He raised his other arm, the laser turret exposed, and a bright beam of collimated light lanced out, striking Steele's machine pistol attachment with pinpoint precision before he could open fire. It melted and fused into a useless polymer/ceramic lump. Steele released the lock and let the attachment fall as the 10mm. gun barrel built into his right forearm came sliding out the gunport in his palm. He had loaded his built-in magazine with armor-piercing bullets. As Stalker brought the laser up, sweeping it along Steele's body toward his head, Steele fired one round after another, emptying the magazine, his target designator locked onto Stalker's turret. The armor-piercing rounds smashed unerringly into Stalker's hand, pulverizing it, smashing the laser turret and rendering it useless.

Stalker screamed and launched himself at Steele.

Steele barely had time to stick his wrist back into his nysteel and polymer hand attachment, snapping it loose from its locking disc on his belt, before Stalker was on him. Steele felt the powerful nysteel arms encircle him and squeeze as they both fell backward to the ground. He rolled, taking Stalker with him, and drove his forehead hard into the renegade cyborg's face, shattering his nose and splintering the cheekbones. For a second, his grip on him loosened and Steele broke free, rolling to his feet.

Stalker came up bellowing and came at him once again. They traded punishing blows. Steele caught one on his chest and felt his nysteel ribs buckle, threatening to crush the human organs underneath. He drove his fist into Stalker's face and saw the jaw break loose, teeth and bone and reinforcing metal disintegrating in a spray of blood. They rained blows on each other, blocking them with their arms, using their powerful nysteel legs in martial arts techniques. Sparks flew as metal met metal and electricity raced from damaged circuits.

Around them, outside the rink, trees and bushes burned, lighting up the sky. Blood poured from Steele's mouth and broken nose. It flowed from Stalker's shattered jaw. Exposed nysteel caught the reflection of the flames. Steele kept trying to block the punches Stalker aimed at his head and chest. One arm now hung useless at his side. He struck out desperately with his foot, using all the force that he could muster in a sidekick aimed at Stalker's knee. The kick connected and the nysteel joint snapped. Stalker went down.

Steele leaped upon him, battering away repeatedly at Stalker's head with his one good hand. The optics cracked and shattered, fracturing like marbles. Stalker's head looked misshapen, dented. He made attempts to block the blows, but Steele kept hammering away relentlessly, like a man possessed, grunting with the effort, smashing away again and again and again. Stalker's arms were flailing now. Sparks shot from his shattered eyes. A hideous, metallic croaking sound came from his throat, but Steele would not let up.

His arm rose and fell and rose and fell repeatedly, smashing through the skull casing even as the impacts broke his nysteel fingers, and the jagged edges of Stalker's broken skull casing sliced through the polymer skin. Electricity crackled like Fourth-of-July sparklers as Steele crashed his battered and misshapen hand into Stalker's cybernetic brain, pounding it to pieces. Stalker was no longer moving. The machine was dead. But Steele kept pounding away until he finally realized, with a shock, that it was over. Then he stopped and stared, horror-struck, at his handiwork.

He had won. And he was not supposed to win. Stalker had been more advanced. Superior in every way. Yet he had won. Something deep within him, something human and indomitable, had allowed him to prevail against all odds. The ruined thing beneath him no longer looked even remotely like a person. It was not Mick Taylor, Steele tried to tell himself. It had never been Mick Taylor. It was machine, much more of a machine than he was, more advanced, more indestructible . . . and yet he had somehow managed to destroy it.

And as he stared at its remains, the memory came back to him of what they had said to each other back in the concourse.

"Come back with me, Mick. Please. Let me help you. They can fix it."

"No! I don't want to be like this! Why couldn't they let me die?"

Steele fell back onto the ground with a moan.

"Oh, God," he said hoarsely. "Why, Mick? *Why*?"

The flames burned brightly around the rink and Steele could hear the sounds of choppers approaching. He thought of Cory, crying out for him as they shot her down. He thought of his son, Jason, close to tears and crying out, "You were never there!" He thought of Janice, saying, "I didn't want the kids to have some kind of robot for a father." And he thought of Mick, crying out, *I don't want to be like this!*

The cry seemed to echo through his mind. And suddenly, he understood and the park echoed with his scream of pain.

_ EPILOGUE _____

Oliver Higgins, Jennifer Stone and Dev Cooper stood in a small room inside the project labs, looking down at the battered body of Lt. Donovan Steele. The damage was staggering, but he was still alive, though he did not know they were there. He was on downtime. When they had picked him up, he was despondent and almost incoherent. He kept mumbling at them to leave him alone, to let him lie there, to go away and let him die.

"You can fix him, can't you?" Higgins said.

Jennifer Stone sighed and compressed her lips in a tight grimace. "Yes, we can fix him," she said. "But it'll take a while. And it's going to cost. I don't know if we've got enough left in our budget to cover the expense."

"You let me worry about that," said Higgins. "I'll find the money somewhere. Just get him back together, I don't care what it takes."

"You're the boss," she said. "I'll start assembling the team. I've managed to recover most of Gates' records. It isn't all there, but there's enough to get the job done and maybe even make a few improvements. You give me enough time and enough money, and I'll have him back as good as new."

"I doubt it," said Dev Cooper.

"Why?" asked Higgins, frowning at him.

Cooper looked a wreck, but for a change, for the first time
in a long time, he was sober. His hands still trembled, and his
body still had a long way to go to recover from what he had put
it through, but he swore that if it killed him, he would never
take another drink again.

"As good as new?" said Dev. "He killed the man who was
once his partner and best friend. He's lost his son again,
probably for good this time, and he had to watch his daughter
die. You really think you can get him back as good as new?"

"We'll get him back," said Higgins. "He'll survive it."

"I wish I could be as sure as you are," Dev said. "But I'm
not. I'm no longer sure of anything."

"I'll have you back as good as new, as well, before I'm
through with you," said Higgins. "I'm going to need you,
Cooper, but I don't need you maudlin and suffering DTs. It
might not be as easy as it will be with Steele, because I can't
have you reprogrammed, but I'll do my best. I figure I owe you
at least that much."

"What do you mean, reprogrammed?" Dev asked.

"He doesn't have to live with the kind of massive guilt
you're talking about," said Higgins. "We can make him forget.
Forget his ex-wife, forget Jason, forget Cory. Forget Stalker.
Forget he had to do what he did. Just wipe the slate clean."

"You can't do that," Dev said.

"I think we can," said Jennifer. "We've learned a lot about
the engram matrix since Gates first assembled it. If we know
what we're looking for, we should be able to isolate specific
memory engrams and block them."

"You can't," said Dev, astonished at their attitude. "You
don't have that right!"

"Well, you're the psychotherapist, Doctor," Higgins said.
"You tell me. If you had a choice between removing a patient's
pain or forcing him to live with it and suffer for the rest of his
life, what would *you* do?"

"It's not that simple," Dev said.

"It is for me," said Higgins. "When we bring him back on
line, he won't remember any of this. There's no reason why he
should. And if I'm ever going to get the project back on track

again, I'm going to need him at one hundred percent. We'll let him forget. He won't know what happened."

"He'll have gaps," said Dev. "Gaps in his life he won't be able to account for. You just can't block important memories like that! Besides, Raven will know. And Ice will know. *I'll* know."

"Yes, but you won't tell him," Higgins said. "And neither will they."

"You're so damn sure of yourself, aren't you?" Dev said. "Only you're forgetting one thing. The backup matrix. The other Steele. The one that left my apartment through the phone lines and integrated with the copy you had. *He'll* know. He's here somewhere, probably listening to every word we're saying, and you can't even find him. What are you going to do about *him*?"

Higgins took a deep breath and let it out slowly. "I don't know. At least, not yet. But I can do something about *this* Steele. When it comes to the matrix, I guess we'll just have to wait and see. Don't worry. We'll find it and we'll get it back under control."

"Maybe," said Dev. "But what if it finds you first?"

They stared at him.

"It can travel through the power lines," said Dev. "It can go through phone circuits. And that means it can go just about anywhere it wants to. Think about it."

He walked out and softly closed the door.